Title

Lia Ramsay

Dedication/Acknowledgments

This story is for my family. Thanks also to my Aunt Brandie for her ideas and editing work.

Chapter 1 – Would You Sell Your Lifespan?

"If you knew exactly how long your life was going to be, would you give up some of your spare years to another person? Say your little sister got cancer and your grandma offered her remaining thirty years to save her – could you begrudge that? No, you couldn't. That would be heroic, right? Grandma had lived a long and fulfilling enough existence and was now ready to pass in exchange for your sister. A sad day for sure, but an honourable choice, right? This is something I grapple with daily. I was born with cancer and never met my grandparents because they traded their lifespans to extend mine. I'm not unique or special in this world. Lots of people are the product of sacrifice; on some level we all are, but more specifically, only some get life sacrificed to them . . ." My voice trailed off when I caught the shrine to my grandparents out of the corner of my eye. I wanted to cry, but even though I admired them greatly, I just didn't know them well enough to be sad.

I looked down at the voice recorder app on my phone as if it would tell me how to continue. Above the app's screen were my phone's dwindling battery meter and a bar that stated fifty years – the amount of time my grandparents had secured for me before I'd need to obtain more or face cancer with a vengeance. The thought spurred my resolve to finish my recorded high school essay on MiraiCorp.

"One hundred years ago, MiraiCorp CEO Falco Jankins devised the brilliant technology to transfer lifespans known as ImmortanWire, which allowed two or more people to transfer their physical vitality from one person to another. Its function is buried under millions of layers of trademarks and secrecy, but suffice it to say, I and many others are proof that it works." My phone beeped a battery alert drawing a look of ire. I saved what little I'd recorded, plugged my phone in, and headed to my wardrobe to put on PJs for the night. Passing my mirror, I caught sight of myself: tall and thin, but with piercing blue eyes and full blonde hair.

"Falco Lyuuda James, you come down here now!" my mom hollered out from the kitchen downstairs. Nervously, I gathered myself, then headed down for what I assumed would be the lecture of a lifetime by the sound of her voice.

"Explain to me why your teacher says your work is average at best? These grades are terrible!" Mom rushed out while angrily thrusting a report card at me. I took the paper, pretending to read it so I could avoid the vitriolic look Mom was giving me. Nevertheless, I found myself glancing into her saddened eyes and tried to ignore the scars on her face.

"Don't shy away like you always do, look at me!" Mom demanded. She was short and too thin, with scars all over her body.

"Why do I have these scars?" she asked pointedly.

"From work accidents that happened at one of your four factory jobs . . ." I said sadly, knowing full well what was coming next.

"Exactly, and why do I work so hard?" she demanded.

"To buy me time . . ."

"Falco, it feels like I say this once a week, but you have to apply yourself or your family's sacrifices will be for naught. I didn't name you after MiraiCorp's first CEO just for you to live an average existence then die of cancer. I wanted you to be the next great CEO!" Mom was becoming exasperated.

I felt guilty. *But it's not my fault I'm nothing special . . . How could I be the next CEO of MC? I'm just me!*

"I'm sorry," I whispered. She was right; I certainly wasn't on track to be rich or anything like that. Yet both Mom and my grandparents gave up so much so I could stand there with a stupid, sad look on my face bereft of wise ideas. Without a word, I grabbed my backpack and stormed out of the house, ignoring Mom's calls. I needed air so I could think.

I jogged out of our cul-de-sac, past our neighbours' identical tan bungalows as I headed for the city. Five minutes later, I reached the city limits near a homeless encampment that was all but abandoned. My friend Joe sat outside the once-bustling encampment in his black electric wheelchair, fiddling with a dream catcher he had tied to its armrest.

Joe was an old First Nations fellow, a proud last-generation veteran of the Water wars, back when traditional wars were still a thing. Nowadays, patriotic heroes simply gave up their lifespans to politicians of their choice to extend whatever their preferred image of democracy was insofar as what that politician represented.

"Hey, Joe!" I said, trying to sound cheery. "Where is everybody?"

Joe coughed. "Know how the MC got into selling TVs?" he began.

"Ya..."

"Well, some MC d-bags came calling with sacks of money, told everybody they'd purchase their lifespans for $500,000 a pop. Gave 'em a day to spend it before they'd cash in."

I wish I could say I was as appalled as Joe sounded, but I wasn't. Maybe it was the generational difference between us. Joe liked to tell me of the times before ImmortanWire, how everyone was dying of an airborne virus sent out by China into their own population first so they wouldn't look guilty, and of how he had enlisted with the Marines to fight the Chinese. Looking at the old, frail, smoker's cough-ridden, tortured man before me, I wasn't sure if I believed his stories. If they were true, Joe would have to be hundreds of years old. I knew what zeta covid was, and I studied the Water wars in school, so if Joe wasn't lying, he'd have lived a tragic life. Supposedly, a few of his squad mates with PTSD were the first to trial ImmortanWire long before it had that name and had given him their lives rather than be tortured by PTSD anymore.

"Needless to say, you refused," I said, genuinely happy, since as destitute as he was, Joe was the best friend I didn't deserve.

"You're damn right!" he wheezed. "Davy, Jane, and Salazar would haunt me if they knew I threw away their lifespans for a quick buck!" Joe pulled out his phone and showed me his lifespan meter. It read one year. My eyes instantly teared up.

"No way, you don't get to die on me, old man!" I said sadly. He just smiled.

"Our society's too dang focused on who gets to live forever, forgetting that dying is a blessing. It means you've done enough, been used enough, and fought enough. I don't look like much now, but dying with dignity is the best middle finger I can give to all the rich leeches that so many died for." He gestured at the empty encampment as an example.

I wanted to cry, but I knew Joe would just punch me for it. I knew he was right. I'd heard the stories of homelessness and drug use being all but eradicated while various CEOs partied into the weekend to celebrate generous lifespan donations. No one could prove they'd paid off the desperate and downtrodden among us; to do so was highly illegal, but we all knew that was what was happening.

"Right now, Billy and Suzie will be out bangin' and partying till their IW appointments tomorrow," Joe said sadly. "Guess I'll be seein' 'em soon enough . . ."

"Joe . . ." I began, but I lost my words.

"Get outta here, kid. Be the one to expose all this bull so our old days of warring weren't for nothin'!"

Sadly, I did as he bid, opting to head for the city as originally intended.

Few people roamed the streets at this hour, as most preferred the lap of luxury that hovercars provided. I glanced up past the sun to the skyscrapers that dotted the skyline. I began to feel a chill through my now dusty PJs and regretted my impulsive decision to storm off unprepared. All I had in my backpack were my tablet and some leftover snacks. That would have to do for now.

I lived on the outskirts of Toronto, a once-bustling city that, besides the hovercars, looked more like a concrete ghost town. I remembered a lecture in health class where the teacher all but begged us to procreate, to a sea of giggles. She was very serious, though. Like Japan of old, humanity's birth rate had declined to a scary degree. Why have children with all the expense and work that it entails when you can just pay off some bum for her lifespan?

All around me, the old skyscrapers acted as billboards for digital advertising, mostly for MiraiCorp since they owned almost everything these days, save for the bigger media companies thanks to monopoly lawsuits. I saw an ad depicting a person with their head in their hands that actually said, *Had enough? Sell your remaining lifespan and be a hero to your family!* The fine print read *$500,000 per sacrifice, limit one per family, plus tax.* And in even smaller print was *Taxes equal to portion of lifespan directly to MiraiCorp for distribution.*

Disgusted, I turned and saw another ad that showed a baby covered in medical equipment. That ad read, *Compassionate sale, up to $1,000,000 per child,* then a phone number for MC Affairs. That made me queasy; I could've been one of those babies sold to some MC CEO to make my mom temporarily well off. But she told them to eat it, and my grandparents chose sacrifice so I could be here today, listlessly wandering through the city with no real goal besides avoiding my mom.

Seeing that ad made me feel guilty for not being better, smarter, richer, something. I shuffled along, wondering how I could remedy that when noise from an alley caught my attention. I could see some thugs harassing someone, but not who. I snuck forward and saw a small disabled kid!

"Why don't you sell your lifespan to us, kid? What are you really using it for at this point?" one lady said. The kid began to cry.

"Hey now, don't cry, little guy . . . just write your name here, then your dad will be safe and rich!" a man said, too happily.

I was in awe. Not because of the thugs, everyone knew shakedowns were common practice among lesser minds, but because a disabled kid actually existed in the city. It took a strong will to raise a disadvantaged child in our world when it looked so much more compassionate, plus was more profitable, to sell the kid's potential lifespan and be done with it.

"You get on outta here!" A booming voice echoed off the walls, then moments later, a huge man with a baseball bat stormed over to accost the thugs. I decided then in my infinite wisdom that a scrawny nobody like me could help, so I rushed over.

"Hey! Leave the kid alone!" I yelled, taking a lame swing at the nearest thug. He dodged my effort easily and kneed me in the gut hard. I went down like a ton of bricks. My vision was awash with sparkly darkness as I was repeatedly kicked in the head.

"Oh no you don't!" I heard as the thug jumped over me toward the big man with the bat who was struggling with the other thug. As I faded out, all I could hear was the crunch of wood against bone amongst screams and wailing.

I awoke later to the sound of rushing feet and machines beeping alerts. I opened my eyes to find myself in a hospital bed with my vision partially obscured by gauze.

"Falco, don't move, you're not fine!" I heard my mom say. My head was pounding and I felt woozy.

Gingerly, I turned my head to see the big man from the alley sitting next to my bed, smiling.

"The name's Steven," he began. "I wanted to say thanks for trying to help my kid back there. I was busy taking a leak in that alley, so the thugs paid me no mind till I whipped out my bat."

"No problem, although it seems you had to help me more than I helped you . . ." I said sadly.

Steven laughed. "You're a good soul, kid. Anyway, I gotta go; kid's waiting at home. Peace!" With that, the big man left, leaving me alone with my vibrating mother. I could tell from her eyes she couldn't decide between being concerned, terrified, or enraged, but she was relieved to see me.

After a while all, she said was, "Never run away from home again!" in a quiet but serious tone.

"Okay, sorry," I said, crying despite my head pain. Mom just held my hand.

After a few days of bedrest, I was encouraged to exercise some, so I began to wander the building. On my way to the bathroom, I passed the infant ward. What I saw there made me deeply uncomfortable: suits all over the place hovering over new parents. Some looked happy to be bothered, doubtless they'd had the child for the purposes of selling it, but others looked stony or dismayed.

That could've been me . . . I thought, while eyeing a sad-looking baby with wires all over it. *What would I do if I were a parent? Granted, I hate kids, but could I really sell one? And if not, if the kid was sick, could I be as brave as my grandparents?* I walked away briskly to the bathroom as if the suits were sharks circling me instead of the newborn babies.

Once I finished in the bathroom, I opened the door to a crying nurse.

"Hi, are you okay?" I asked.

"They're not all sick," she said as she sobbed, gesturing down the hall, then gasped and slammed her mouth closed.

"I won't tell. What do you mean?"

She debated telling me for a moment before her emotions broke her attempt at a façade of rule-enforced silence. "The hospital *might* be paid off to *maybe* falsify diagnoses so MC bigwigs can swoop in and buy the children's lifespans without the families feeling guilty," she whispered quickly to me.

I felt enraged by the very prospect she was describing, making my aching head swim. "Can you prove this?" I asked calmly, thinking back to Joe and how he'd want to take the hospital and MC down for such transgressions. Babies were a hot commodity because you'd get their entire lifespan, not just what little was left, like in the case of an adult.

"No!" she sobbed, then pushed past me into a bathroom stall to cry.

On my way back to my room, I mulled over what she'd said; it didn't overly surprise me if true. Every CEO and bigwig from every successful company on the planet wanted more life to fuel their selfish legacies and maintain their control. MiraiCorp's CEO had it made because every lifespan transaction came with taxes in the form of some life going to him, meaning he could effectively live youthfully and strong for as long as ImmortanWire stayed in use. *No one should live as long as him, it's wrong, especially if that nurse is right about the exploitative means he's using.*

When I got back to my room, Mom came in and handed me my phone that I'd left at home. I was dismayed to find my beating had shaved two precious years off my lifespan. *Sorry, Grandma and Grandpa . . .* I thought sadly. Now I only had forty-eight years left to become someone big. *And feed into this vicious cycle of life stealing.* Could I really stomach that? Me, as I am, could I really take someone else's life to further my own? I highly doubted it. Maybe I'd be more like Joe and graciously get old. However, I wasn't near death, so it was impossible to say what I would or wouldn't do in the heat of the moment. I resolved to be brave like my mother and banished the thought.

Chapter 2 – We Might Live in a Society

Once I was discharged and back home, I picked up my guitar and began to play. Music helped me focus at the worst of times. While I played, all I could think about were the advertisements in the city as well as what the nurse had secretly told me. It was then, as I tossed my journal aside, I knew what I wanted: I want to help people. The best way someone like me could stick it to MC and other like-minded corporations would be to use my experiences to help people that want to live! If I could get a job in the hospital, then I might also be able to find that nurse or otherwise find evidence against MC. I'd need help. Thankfully, I knew just the man: Joe.

I got dressed and headed to the homeless encampment. I was happy to see Joe had neighbours, since a new group of homeless people had moved in. *Sucks to see people so downtrodden, but if that nurse is right, I'll need an army.*

"Hey, Joe, I know you're short on time but hear me out: I want to take down the MC d-bags. The people here tend to respect you; can you convince them not to sacrifice themselves and is there anyone here who can help me to infiltrate Criton hospital and get proper evidence?" I asked breathlessly.

Joe's eyes lit up. "Where's this coming from?" he asked.

"I met someone important who said that MC is paying extra to falsify babies' diagnoses to help gain their CEO lifespan."

Joe looked ready to fight. "I think I know just the person, follow me!"

He led me deeper into the encampment than I'd ever been. We came up to a disheveled woman in a tattered business suit who walked right up to me, extending her hand.

"My name is Liara Yulee," she said, shaking my hand firmly. I was shocked.

"Cousin of MiraiCorp's current CEO Jansen Yulow?" I asked.

"Yes," she affirmed.

"I read that you were disowned by your family; I never expected to see you here!"

She took a deep breath. "I overheard my father gloating about all the life he'd obtained from lying to new parents. I threatened to expose him, was abducted by his goons who forcibly siphoned off most of my lifespan, then tossed out, disowned, and disinherited by the family." Her hair was grey and she looked seventy-five, even though she was supposed to be in her thirties.

"Why are you telling me this?" I asked.

"She tells everyone who will listen," Joe piped up. "I didn't put much stock in it myself until you came calling. Now I'm interested."

"And you are?" she asked.

"Falco James. I want to take down MC and stop the corruption!" I stomped my foot emphatically.

"Do you have a plan?" she asked me.

Nervously, I smiled. *Am I out of my depth here?* "I've been accepted to Jinchou University, the Masters in Counseling program. I'll become an end-of-life counselor to expose and stop the corruption from the inside, deny MC more lives! I may have a contact who might be able to help me get evidence against Criton and MC."

"Might?" She was unconvinced.

"Yes."

Liara mulled my plan over for a moment. "I like you, kid. I take it you want to be CEO when all's said and done?"

"No, ma'am, you can."

"Alright. It's a plan. Joe and I will try to keep people around on our end, and out of MC hands, while you focus on school. I have some funds that my family doesn't know about, so how about I pay for your dorm while you study?" she suggested.

"Wow, thanks!" I said, shaking her hand. *If she ends up CEO, it'll be chump change for her, but it's still a nice offer.*

In the early days, I met with Joe once a week so he could teach me Marine espionage tactics, how to keep my cool under pressure, handle a weapon, and self-defence. Or sort of self-defence; it's rather difficult in my condition. I'd long since finished high school and was deep into my Master's. During which time,

I made a point of getting to know the homeless in Joe's encampment, and many helped by letting me practise on them. I think together we helped some find reason again, if only for a little while.

Unfortunately, Joe's time came due. He passed on a warm sunny day in June surrounded by friends. In his handwritten will he left me his pistol and the silly dreamcatcher he kept hanging on his armrest. I cried for days. The last thing he said to me was, "Don't forget your mission. Make us count!"

It took two agonisingly slow years before I got my Masters in Counseling to become an end-of-life counsellor. Without Mom's hard work saving for my post-secondary education and Liara's secret donation, I wouldn't have made it. I think I finally managed to make Mom somewhat proud in the process. Sure, being a counsellor is no CEO level job, but it seemed honourable enough in her eyes and was a fulfilling goal for me to chase. I suppose she figured I could still end up CEO of the hospital or something far-fetched like that.

I never forgot my true goals by any stretch of the imagination, but post-secondary was pleasant enough except for the times when I'd watch the news. In one newscast, MiraiCorp's CEO was bragging about amassing 900 years in total lifespan. *How many babies died for that?* I wondered contemptuously. *This can't continue!* I doubled my resolve. All work and little sleep made me a dull boy.

Finally, I was finished! I was overjoyed to be back home with Mom, who was watching the news. A bulletin went off, showing the picture of the nurse from the hospital. I was captivated.

"Thirty-three-year-old Enriqua Sollis was found dead in her apartment this morning, a gunshot to the head. Witnesses tell CRBN News Sollis was distressed the night before. She had been embroiled in a four-year-long legal battle with Criton Hospital and MiraiCorp wherein she alleged falsified documentation led to illegitimate lifespan transfers predominantly from babies. MiraiCorp representatives and hospital spokespeople continue to deny any and all wrongdoing, citing a lack of evidence. We remind citizens that all IW transfers come with a tax, benefiting MiraiCorp – check your contract. CRBN News is brought to you by MiraiCorp. More news at ten."

I was flabbergasted. There she was, my one hope for an ally, and she was dead. People were very rarely murdered these days, as it was much easier to strong-arm someone into "donating" their lifespans via other means. To be murdered was to be correct; at least it was to me. Someone really wanted to shut the poor healthcare hero up. I was dismayed and walked upstairs to my room so Mom wouldn't notice my expression. I never told her about that nurse at the hospital years ago, and I couldn't explain it now. Better for her to think a nurse inspired me to get into healthcare and that's all there was to it. Now more than ever, I was excited for my job interview tomorrow.

The Next Day

I sat in the Criton Hospital's Head of the Mental Health department with my resume and Master's in hand.

"Falco Lyuuda James, I'm Susan Hyruda, come in!" Susan wore a smart business suit with an expression that made her look wise beyond her years. Though that could just be because she'd lived longer than her body could show.

"I just have a few questions for you if you're ready to begin?" she said.

"Absolutely!" I said, smiling.

"Okay: What do you consider the major causes of mental health issues nowadays, especially when we speak about people in our hospital?"

"A lack of self-worth and no sense of identity. We live in a world where life itself is a commodity."

"How did you deal with a difficult situation, or help with an unhappy patient?"

"My friend died and I coped by seeking help from a social worker. To help unhappy patients, I'd empathize, before forwarding them to their doctor."

"What do you consider the toughest aspect of this job?"

"Convincing people that their life is worth living."

"How do you feel about receiving a luxury holiday voucher from the sales representative of one of the pharma companies?"

"That would be abhorrent; I'd never accept such nonsense."

"How do you plan to build trust with the patients?"

"I always try to remain honest, fair, and transparent to gain patient trust."

Susan smiled. "Thank you, Mr James, I'll take your paperwork. When can you start?"

"Today!" I said eagerly, drawing a laugh from her.

"We'll be in touch," she said, shaking my hand before gesturing to the door.

After an agonizing week of waiting, I received a call informing me I'd got the job, starting today.

"Mom, I did it! I'm now hired at Criton!" I exclaimed.

"Woohoo!" Mom hollered. We hugged, then I left to go to work. For the next few months, it was business as usual, though I never forgot my true goal: expose Criton and MiraiCorp. The only problem was, I had no idea where to begin. *Some secret agent I am . . .*

I wanted to start by befriending the nurses in the maternity department of the hospital. With the passing of Enriqua, everyone there was hush-hush, not at all keen on talking to some overly eager counselor. I was delighted when one of her old friends agreed to meet me for coffee one evening. She went by Sandra, though the way she said her name made me think it wasn't really her name. Regardless, I was excited.

We met at *Paul's Cafe*, a rustic place built in an old house with wood panelling along the walls and '50's era bench seats separated by small tables with galaxies emblazoned on them. *Paul's* was empty, so the two of us kept it pretty quiet.

"Hi, Sandra, thanks for meeting with me. I met Enriqua briefly some time ago, and what she said spurred me into action. I don't want anything to happen to you, I'm just trying to get information and some proof," I began.

"Look, I can't stay and I want nothing to do with whatever Enriqua was involved in! She left me this." She passed me a flash drive under the table then continued, "She told me I was supposed to give it to the news if anything happened to her, but, again, I don't want to be involved. Whatever you do with it is on you! Good luck!" With that, she nervously smiled, hugged me, and left.

Now it was just Paul and me. I knew he had been watching us, and I couldn't help but feel nervous. I drank my coffee and headed home for the night, fisting the flash drive in my pocket until I could find something to do with it.

The next day was work as usual, thinking little of my interaction with Sandra until I got home.

"What in the world? Another one!" Mom gasped at the news on TV as I passed, heading to my room. I turned on the news and felt my blood drain from my face. There, on the news, was Sandra's face, or Lucy Turm as it turned out her name really was; she too had been shot. I rushed downstairs and hugged my mom, trying not to shake with fear.

"I love you," I said.

"What's the matter?!" Mom demanded. "Was she a friend of yours?"

"Something like that. Things are just getting too real, Mom," I said.

"You're not mixed up with these nurses, are you? Better not be." My mom's facial expression froze me.

"No, I'm not, Mom," I lied, hoping the flash drive wouldn't burn a hole in my pocket and expose me.

I sat with Mom a bit then went to my room; I had to see what was on the flash drive. There were documents detailing the thousands of cumulative years MC bigwigs had siphoned off from the taxes. *Nothing illegal there,* I thought to myself, but kept scanning. Then I saw the corporate memos and hospital emails indicating extra compensation. I had all the proof I needed in writing. But it was all old, so MC could easily say those people no longer worked at the company. I stashed the flash drive away and decided to head back to the hospital.

Once there, I started digging through patient files until a huge man approached me from behind, sticking a gun in my back.

"Cease your digging or die," was all he said before he left me there shaking.

I can't. I won't, I thought, inwardly cursing myself for leaving Joe's pistol at home. I gathered any files where people alleged in detail the MC coercion, then headed home.

There I matched my makeshift testimony from distraught parents with dates on the drive. What I saw appalled me: hundreds of lives were erroneously sacrificed for massive kickbacks based on created diagnoses. MC's iron-clad nondisclosure agreements, which I'd never seen before, left me to console the peo-ple who'd rather die than live should they learn the truth.

Enraged, I anonymously posted some of my findings, secured the flash dri-ve into my pants pocket, and went to bed.

At work the next day, Susan Hyruda called me into her office. Nervously I at-tended, unsure of what this could mean.

"Ma'am . . ." I said, politely.

"Take a seat, Falco." She gestured to the chairs beside the police officer. My nerves were going crazy. *Why is the cop here?! I wish I never took this flash drive!* I thought, cursing myself inwardly.

"Mr James, I'm sorry to be the one to tell you this, but your mother's been murdered," the stocky officer said.

"What?! How?" I demanded.

The officer looked apologetic. "Looks like a robbery gone wrong. Your mother was shot."

"W-was anything stolen?" I stammered.

"At this time, we don't know. We're sorry for your loss." The officer left me there crying in my boss's office. I felt ashamed, stupid, and guilty. *Was this my fault? Did I ask too many questions?*

"Take a couple weeks off, Falco. Your job will still be here when you're ready," Susan said gently.

I had to sell everything Mom had to scrounge up almost enough money to bury her. Thankfully, her friends helped me out. I barely remember the proceed-ings; it's all a blur of tears and a profound sense of guilt. *No one gets murdered anymore, unless they cross the MC.* I cried harder, resigned to defeat. Slumping down on the empty floor, I felt something hard pressing against my leg, jarring me from my pained stupor. It was the damned flash drive. I pulled it from my pocket, debating whether or not to snap it in half when a calm washed over me. *No, I want revenge! And this is gonna give it to me!*

Slipping it back in my pocket, I hurried to the nearest hovercab station. I rode to CRBN News headquarters, walked up to the nearest investigative journalist based on his desk plaque, and handed him the drive.

"The hell is this now?" he asked; the plaque said his name was Murphy Smith.

"This, Mr. Smith, is proof MC and Criton hospital are colluding to falsify diagnoses and forge justification for parents to sell their newborns' lifespan to MC bigwigs!" I stated quietly.

Mr. Smith eyed me carefully, like he was measuring me up. "Big news, if true. And you got this where exactly?" he asked skeptically, but I could see excitement in his eyes.

"From the recently deceased Lucy Turm, friend of Enriqua Sollis," I said.

Still eyeing me carefully, he held the drive as if it were really hot. For a moment, I was sure he was dismissing me out of hand, but instead he plugged the drive in and began browsing. I watched as his eyes widened and a Cheshire grin spread across his face.

"So, she wasn't just a kook after all . . ." he finally said. Then his expression hardened. "What do you want for this?" he asked like a businessman ready to play hardball.

I shrugged nonchalantly. "Nothing. Just justice for the countless number of victims this scheme has killed worldwide, including my mom, Jane," I said seriously.

"But what I want to know is why now? Why pass this thing along when she could've presented it herself ages ago?" he asked rhetorically.

I shrugged. "Doubtless she was under a lot of stress, and she was a public figure so maybe it took until it was too late for her to get this. I can't say, I didn't know her."

"Anyway, thanks for this Mr . . .?"

"No problem, Mr. Smith, go get 'em!" I said, waving as I backed out of there without giving my name, then hailed another cab, heading for a hotel. I couldn't bear going home; nothing was left for me there. I checked my phone. To my horror, three years of my lifespan were gone. *Stress . . . Sorry . . . Grandparents . . . again. If I end up dead soon, I'll apologise in person.* I smiled ruefully.

Feeling relieved the information was finally out there, I went to sleep with Joe's pistol at my side, and never heard the gunshot that killed me.

Chapter 3 – Murphy Smith – One Hour Earlier

I was blown away by the memos and hospital documents he left me. It didn't take much leg work to track down who he was. Falco James, the man himself of no significance, but the information he brought me – wow! I immediately set about publishing an exposé that hit the web before my shift ended. I didn't know if I'd be next on the chopping block, so I opted to sleep at work under my desk surrounded by security cameras. Journalists are odd and sometimes work late, so no one questioned my choices. I awoke to find my colleagues all shouting for joy and some in revulsion at my work. When it came across the wires that Falco James was found dead, by gunshot in a hotel, I added his name to the victims' section of the exposé. The news quickly went global.

My boss, George, called me into his office.

"Smith!" he started. "What in all the hells?"

"Right?" I said with a touch of professional sadness.

"You just had this under your belt and said nothing?!"

"It was only delivered to me yesterday by Falco James. Then he was killed, boss, no secrets here."

"Jesus . . . Well, heads are rolling at MC branches worldwide and Criton hospital is now under investigation!"

George was a portly man with a white beard. We jokingly called him Santa. His office was a broom closet full of manilla folders with a single tiny desk, but the look on his face told me this story would bring us all a raise . . . or death. Whatever the case, he was cautiously happy, so I was too.

"Do you think anything will change?" I asked with a hint of naive optimism.

"Nah, supposedly one bastard got canned but just took a cushy HR job at another branch. A single story does not a real empire crumble. Though you shook foundations the world over, don't get me wrong, it's a long way from right. And the formerly banished Liara Yulee has been instituted as Toronto branch CEO. She's promising sweeping reforms; we'll see," he said, deep in thought, and turned his chair toward the windows.

"Great . . ." I said. *I hope this was the ending you wanted, Mr James!*

In a vault room somewhere deep under the city a person sat shrouded in shadow. From within the shadow an old hand reached out for a nearby hourglass and flipped it over.

"Leader?" A voice asked.

"Jankins is out of the picture, it's time." The elder voice said. The speaker rose from a high-back chair into the light of an ornate desk lamp to reveal a black mask with a golden hourglass in its center. The speaker clapped and lights engaged in the ceiling revealing a room full of people all in suits with black masks. The Leader walked slowly past the crowd of onlookers to a set of ImmortanWire chairs with knight's armour behind them. The Leader sat in one while the man he spoke to previously bowed to him before sitting in the other.

"Your sacrifice will ensure a new world order!" The Leader said resolutely then nodded to a mask-clad woman in a black dress whom stood by a lever. On his go, the woman pulled the lever and the ImmortanWire system engaged. In seconds the sacrificial man's body shriveled up like a raisin as his last breath rattled free of his lips.

Moments later the Leader stood anew, his muscles bulging under his old-timey black suit. While straightening his tie he gestured to the dead man beside him.

"Ensure his children are taken care of and are made keenly aware the importance of his gift this day!"

"Of course, great Leader." the woman said, her voice betraying the grin she wore under her mask.

"On this fateful day, the Keepers, the true descendants of King Artorious, rise again!"

A cheer erupted in the vault-like space. The Leader clasped his hands together menacingly.

"We are all dust in the hourglass of fate. Like a sandstorm we will rage and envelope the world..." The Leader began.

"Blasting away the filth and reclaiming our birthright!" The crowd of masked people chanted.

The Leader waved his hands and the crowd dispersed back to their mundane cover lives, waiting for their fated time to take over the world as their mantra promised them. Only the masked woman remained, waiting for his command.

"Now, about MiraiCorp," he began, "How is the acquisition coming?" he asked, inwardly excited for the answer he knew was coming.

"With Jankins' controlling stake recently legally dissolved and share prices at an all time low, our previous low-ball offer of twenty billion was finally accepted!" she reported happily.

"Good, it would seem we owe Mr. Murphy Smith our favour." The Leader said casually.

"I will scatter some of our Dust to the wind to watch over him."

"Good work my beloved." The Leader sat back at his desk then began to peruse the news, smiling at the disarray reported. *Homelessness is at an all-time high, disease runs rampant, and cost of living has tripled under the current government. All while the rich colonize space rather than help. People will be glad of a new world order!* The Leader mused to himself.

The night crept up behind me while I was lost in my thoughts. The shopping bag on my arm weighed me down more than I'd like to admit. I was getting old and weak. Smiling, I waved off another batch of destitute homeless people panhandling for money. Down a dark alley I could see the side street that connected my cul-de-sac to the road. Thinking nothing of it I opted to take the dreary shortcut. Just as my eyes had adjusted to the darkness I heard heavy boots approaching from behind. I nervously wrapped my trenchcoat around myself then turned to face what I hoped was another homeless person. Two large men approached in very casual loose-fitting garb with ice in their expressions.

"You Murphy Smith?" One asked.

"Yes, how can I help you gentlemen?"

"The CEO sends his regards." the first man said as he drew a silenced pistol and leveled it at my head. I felt myself beginning to shake and closed my eyes, ready for the endless fear of coming retribution to end. But instead of a loud bang sending me into eternal sleep, I vaguely heard gurgling screams followed by two heavy thumps. When I opened my eyes the two men laid in pools of their own blood while a shadowy figure in what looked to be a dinner suit and black mask stood over their bodies. The individual casually wiped his knives off on the dead men's shirts paying no mind to me.

"Who are you?" I managed to stutter still shaking from the whole ordeal.

"Dust." A male-sounding voice responded from behind his strange ornate mask. With that said, as if it answered all the questions in the world, the person bowed to me and scaled a nearby drainpipe on the side of a building, disappearing as quickly as they'd come.

I managed to dial 911, answered their questions, then waited for the police. Once they cut me loose I headed home still visibly shaken. I lived alone in a one bedroom apartment subdivided in a house with three neighbours. In my line of work a family was a liability, or a target for leverage, however one wants to look at it. Corporations rule governments, which in turn stifle the destitute people. I mustered what was left of the shreds of my courage then set about installing hidden cameras and bugs all through my home. If something like what happened tonight found my doorstep, there'd be ample evidence for the police to conveniently ignore before the coroner took my body to the dump or something. I couldn't afford a proper burial or even a cremation. Hell, I could barely afford one room to live in even after George gave me a bonus for breaking the Falco James story. After tonight's events all I could think about was my mysterious savior. The police had all but laughed me off when I mentioned Dust, happy to chock it up as gang-related violence that I happened to witness, and not an attempt on my fragile life!

Since when do gang-bangers run around in full suits with fancy masks assassinating people before casually scaling a building? I Googled ninja assassinations but that only brought up historical tales of the real ninjas of ancient Japan. I tried searching for dust assassins, but that turned up nothing. The image of a pure black ornate mask with what at the time had looked like a painted hourglass shape on it burned through my mind's eye. On a whim I Googled hourglass ninjas and there was many garbage results, mostly pictures of my two search terms, but after scrolling a while I came upon a Google excerpt from a book published ten years ago. The book was titled *The Keepers: A Comprehensive History* by James Sunderland. I read through the excerpt trying to ignore how wild it all sounded long enough to remain objective. *A secret order that once ruled the colonized world, funded by a long-dead ruler who was guarded by a cabal of assassins?!* I thought to myself, shaking my head. *Well, I live in a world where immortality is a thing so why not?* Reviews for the book were resoundingly negative, calling the autobiography a fiction at best, a children's tale a worst. It didn't help matters that researching the author turned up multiple corroborated articles citing that he was a hack conspiracy theorist who unironically believed the world was flat and that white people were being replaced.

Stifling my judgment for the time being I bought the book digitally and spent the rest of my adrenaline-induced sleepless night reading it. I came away from my binge reading mostly disappointed. The book detailed that an order founded by King Artorious in the fifteenth century A.D. believed one day they'd rule the world, and not only did they supposedly achieve this, but they pioneered immortality. The only part that had kept me reading was the mention of the King's Guards royal masks: Ornate black full face coverings with a gold hourglass shape in the center. Supposedly after King Artorious' death his loyal soldiers kept the order alive in secret, calling their leadership the Keepers while there assassins were referred to only as Dust. *Dust... like sand in the hourglass?* I wondered. If this so-called autobiography had any merit its implication that the Keepers and their cabal of assassins still existed made me shiver. *Doubtless if such an old-money system still existed in this world they'd be everywhere, infiltrating every level of authority, just waiting...but for what? This world is too shit to have some secret utopia of a regal leadership running it. And if the King is dead, assuming he was ever real, there goes their immortality claims. But then how do I explain my savior? I help take down the current world order and suddenly someone wearing the symbol of a world order of assassins shows up to save me? They must've just been a copycat.* I thought to myself as I scribbled down notes.

"Just someone with impeccable style playing dress up, maybe some wacko fan of this book?" I muttered to myself. I was grateful to be alive, but wished it wasn't under such mysterious circumstances. I ended up having to call in sick and spent the following day asleep.

The Leader rose from his large desk, removed his mask, and joined his beloved in a nearby elevator.

As they rode she finally spoke, "Well, Mr. Aziz it would seem everything is going your way."

The Leader chuckled wryly, "Indeed Mrs. Aziz it is. Once MC is ours we'll have the capitol for a Prime Ministerial run. Not that the current Prime Minister is likely to disobey us..."

"Of course not. You'll be happy to know the situation with Murphy Smith has been resolved."

"Good, is he likely to be a problem?"

"Internet Service Provider records show he's looking into us, but he won't get any further than Sunderland did."

"We had to kill Sunderland remember?"

"I think Smith will be different."

"In what way?"

"We saved him, maybe we can recruit him."

"We shall see..." The Leader finished as the elevator doors slid opened.

The Aziz' exited the executive elevator, went down a short hallway, through a keycard entrance and into the lobby of Aziz Solar Systems.

Chapter 4 – Shadow Family

The Aziz' walked past a line of schoolchildren touring their facility with warm smiles on their faces. No one would ever know what dealings they hid below. Hand in hand they exited their building, a post-modern skyscraper, and entered a waiting hover-limo which took them home. Their house was a modest two-story bungalow on the outskirts of the city which they purchased one hundred years ago for the lowly some of thirty million when the housing market was down. It wouldn't do for the leader of multiple organizations to be homeless; that fate was best saved for the Dust as it made them cheaper to pay. Two cars waited in the driveway when they pulled up. Mr. Aziz tipped their driver and helped his wife get out. She didn't need the help, he was just oldschool like that.

"Thank you, Rudolfo." she cooed.

"Any time, my love." he responded.

"The children are home!" she said happily.

"Indeed, I look forward to hearing of their adventures!"

The pair entered their home to fine their son, Jonathan, and daughter, Revy sitting on the couch, hands clasped in anticipation of their parents' arrival. Jonathan was roughly twenty in appearance and was built like a football star. He wore a suit not unlike his father's while Revy was a tall, fit woman in jean shorts and a tank top.

"Revy, you know I detest that outfit!" Mrs. Aziz lectured.

"And you know any self-respecting MMA fighter wouldn't be caught dead in a dress!" Revy retorted with a hint of attitude.

Jonathan sighed, "I keep telling you this is why Mother won't hand over business dealings to you, you're too immature... after all this time!"

"And you're a rank daddy's boy!" Revy sneered.

Jonathan tensed, "I'm a blackbelt too, you don't see me wearing a speedo!"

"Alright enough you two..." Rudulfo cautioned. He joined his kids on the couch, putting one arm around each of them. "Tell me of your efforts of late." he commanded with a hint of gentleness. Immediately both siblings became serious. Jonathan began. "I've been promoted to senior scriptwriter for the Prime Minister, sir."

"And I've been accepted into the Secret Service thanks to your recommendation, Dad... I mean sir. Guarding the Deputy PM."

"Perfect, we have Dust infiltrating every level of authority, but I find it comforting you two are so ingratiated to our allies. It means I have little to fear should they become enemies."

"As if you ever get afraid." Revy joked.

"Oh, there was a time, many moons ago, before I met your mother that I was far more uncertain." Rudolfo admitted.

"Back in the days of King Artorious and the fountain of youth, eh?" Revy joked.

Jonathan gave her a look.

Surprising both of them Rudulfo laughed. "Hey, I'm not that old, you brat!"

"Okay, enough business you three, it's almost time for dinner." Mrs. Aziz chided.

"Righto, time for wood! Rudy it's chopping time!" All three smiled as an aging English Mastiff emerged from the living room to dutifully follow Rudulfo into the back yard where piles of wood waited. Jonathan chuckled when Mrs. Aziz held up a hand for silence and on queue Rudolfo broke into song about how much he loved his dog and his family. Like a well-oiled machine, the trio set about preparing dinner while Rudolfo chopped wood to heat the house.

Sweaty of brow, Rudulfo returned to the kitchen with Rudy close behind and took his seat at the head of the table. The family joined hands so Rudulfo could say Grace.

"Lord we give thanks for bringing the family together again, and thanks for our successes in our glorious duty to lead humanity. We give thanks for the roof over our head and the food we are about to receive in the bounty of Christ the Lord, Amen!" Rudulfo concluded smiling.

"Amen!" The family said in unison, Rudy grumbled from the living room drawing giggles from Mrs. Aziz. The family turned to a sound coming from outside their kitchen bay window to find a camouflaged hover-transport pulling into their driveway. Rudulfo's blue eyes became stern. He walked over to the front door right as the driver knocked.

"General Aziz?" The driver, dressed in full military garb asked.

"Yes?" Mrs. Aziz said from behind Rudolfo.

"We have a situation ma'am, I need you to come with us!" The driver said.

"A moment, soldier, I'll be right there." Mrs. Aziz rushed upstairs, swapped her dress for her uniform, and marched out the door dutifully, Leaving Rudulfo to close the door behind her with a worried look on his face. Noticing his expression, Revy put a hand on his shoulder.

"Mom will be fine like always, they probably just need her to coordinate deployment of your solar systems like usual."

"I always fear the Prime Minister will order her to give up her lifespan for hers." Rudolfo admitted sadly, keenly aware of the role of the modern military grunt these days.

Jonathan grimaced but gathered himself, "Mom's too valuable for that, you know that. Besides the Dust will blow her way in defense if need be." he said seriously.

"You know I don't like relying on the Dust..." Rudolfo sighed.

Revy piped up. "Mom trained most of them, at least the local ones, they'll never let anyone harm her."

"I Know!" Rudulfo boomed, a hint of the Leader coming out in his tone. He took a breath and let his bulging muscles relax under his suit. "I just hate leaving her defense to others, she's my beloved. Were something to befall her..." He caught himself, stopping his mind's wandering there.

Jonathan smiled gently. "I'd pity the fool who tried to harm her, sir."

Rudolfo grinned with a hint of menace, his worries assuaged by his son's confidence. *Of course, I'm being a fool, she can match me in battle, no need to worry, but I just can't help myself...* Rudulfo thought. The family went to bed certain all would be well soon.

I woke at my desk to find my display riddled with dead-end research on the mythical children's tale of The Keepers. George hobbled over from his office, took one look at my screen and guffawed.

"Smith, what the hell are you looking into that for, you ain't becoming a conspiracy nut are ya?"

"I'm telling you, George, this conspiracy has some weight to it!" I retorted.

"Why, because some wacko cosplaying a Dust assassin saved your life? Please. I'd sooner believe you took down those men yourself!"

"But I didn't."

"Obviously, ya scrawny lout. Now quit your nappin' and get serious!"

I sat up in my chair. "What's going on?"

George grabbed a remote and turned up the volume on our news TV. My eyes went wide with shock.

The Chinese President flanked by his fellow dictatorial ally in The Russian President were declaring war on the West. The news reports displayed the countless troops and vehicles that the Axis forces had amassed. My mouth fell opened.

"So taking the lifespans of their patriots wasn't good enough anymore huh?" I mumbled to myself.

"Seems that way. Get writing! People need to know the facts, find out what forces we have if you can, that sort of thing." George ordered.

"On it!" I said, closing my research tabs and getting to work. The Keepers would have to wait.

"General Layla Aziz reporting for duty! Madam Prime Minister, the boys filled me in on the gist, would you be so kind as to elaborate?"

"The Chinese and Russians are invading. Everyone here should know that, but what most won't realize is we do not have the troops or manufacturing capacity to respond." The PM began.

Layla knew damn well why not, as her continued life was a part of the problem, so instead she asked, "How bad is it?"

"NORAD is all but destroyed, our remaining air force personnel are routed, and cities are already being bombed." the PM responded sadly.

"Jesus... How can I help?"

"By coordinating a response with the few thousand personnel we have left and by accelerating training of the ... well vagrants who've been volunteering in droves."

"Volunteers... good. How many do we have?"

"Military census data shows about 3000 to date." The PM said.

*So maybe 3000 trained troops and falling, bolstered by 3000 plebs that are likely barely alive. Great...*Layla thought. "I can work with that." she looked around the room at her fellow officials, then continued. "Ma'am, what if I told you I could amass a trained force off the books?"

The PM squinted in thought, "I'll sanction it, anything you can do to help we need."

The Leader would normally greatly abhor this use of his Dust, but if we win it furthers our goals and will greatly ingratiate the world to him. Layla thought with a knowing smile. "With your leave, ma'am..." Layla said. The PM nodded in consent.

Wasting no time, Layla walked into a barren hallway and called Rudolfo over their secure line.

"My love I have a request." she began.

"Related to the war?" his voice boomed from under his mask.

He's underground.... Good. "Yes sir, with your leave I'd like command of our 10,000 local Dust to bolster the Canadian forces and aid me in training new recruits."

"Aziz Solar Systems has already committed personnel and funds to the military. At this time with the coming election on hold, I've instructed my Dust over the dark web to remain underground, metaphorically and literally where possible."

"My love, do you mean to say you can't help me?"

"Negative. I can commit 1000 trained Dust to your cause by way of sudden unmasked volunteers. But I don't see losing all our forces against a greater force as wise."

"Love you needn't remind me of tactics..."

"Then why do you ask so much of me?!" The Leader boomed.

Layla remembered the stroke of his powerful hand on her cheek, and then the feeling of that same hand tightening around her neck. "F-forgive me sir. I mean only to further your glorious God-given purpose! If we win this war your election is a shoe-in!"

"It is so regardless. Take the Dust I offer and spread the grains wisely."

"Yes sir. Are the children with you?"

"Of course."

"Thank you, sir. Goodbye."

Layla gathered her resolve then rejoined the PM and her cohort. "Ma'am my sources say we'll receive 1000 soldiers funded by Aziz Solar Systems."

"Rudolfo has already given billions in support, do thank him for us. Wherever did he find soldiers?" The PM asked suspicious.

"He had connections with mercenaries that ran security for our solar installations in less-than-savory countries." Layla lied.

"Mercs...Perfect, well the more the merrier, do thank him for me!"

"I will, ma'am. I'm off to begin training." Layla said, starting to leave.

"Wait! The Defense Minister said, "Our closest base just got hit. Where should we send the troops?"

Smiling to put her at ease, Layla brought up a map on her phone and forwarded them the address of one of the Aziz warehouses. Which at one point conveniently doubled as a Dust training facility in the long night hours. She saluted the PM, turned and left to her waiting military escort. She quickly texted Rudolfo the address, knowing he'd get the idea, then hopped in the military hover-truck.

When they arrived at the unscathed warehouse so much time had passed night had fallen. Layla smiled to herself, inwardly praising the war-time traffic jams. Leaving her escort outside, Layla buzzed herself in to find people standing throughout the space in perfect rows.

"Like a sandstorm we will rage and envelope the world..." she began.

"Blasting away the filth and reclaiming our birthright!" The crowd of now unmasked people chanted. In unison they all bowed to her regally. Layla smiled, the Dust had blown her way just as the Leader had promised.

"Break with decorum for a time. I permit you all remember your birth names provided you train three people each expediently. Understood?" Layla ordered.

Every speck of Dust saluted like the mercenaries they were posing as. With operating rules established and missions accepted, Layla went back outside with the air of a General to greet the 3000 vagrants now arriving in military hover-trucks.

"I am General Layla Aziz, Canadian Spec Ops. You will obey my people till you become true deadly soldiers, or you will be sent to your deaths at the hands of savage invaders. Choose wisely which you'd prefer, whether you live or die is hereafter in your hands. Come with me!"

Layla opened the truck shipping bay doors so her new recruits could take in her building full of cold-eyed Dust.

"Three trainees per person, split up and get to work now!"

Over the next few weeks the Dust, with supplies and weapons delivered by un-marked military hover-trucks, taught the vagrants to fight and shoot. The basics at least, enough that they could be pointed at an enemy and told to fight, like dumb missiles... Fire and forget. As Canada burned Layla stood resolute. In her mind's eye she pictured a future the Leader promised of a Canada rebuilt, even when she only had 4000 barely ready people to fight with; 3000 of which were mostly just there for the free uniforms and food. On a fine sunny day with explosions booming in the background and the screams of Chinese and Russ-ian jets overhead, Layla mustered her troops.

"I'm loathe to say this so soon, but you're as ready as we can make you. Transports should be arriving soon to take you to the front lines. Dismissed!" *If I'm honest, these plebs are nowhere near ready, but we're running out of time...* Layla thought. In that moment trucks pulled up quickly, surprising her slightly. "Those aren't ours." She said, "GET READY!" Layla grabbed her assault rifle and opened fire on the joint Axis attackers streaming from the trucks. Taking cover inside her cement building Layla watched with her peripheral vision as her new troops fought beside her, dying in droves without cover given the truck bay doors were opened. The air stunk of sulfur, shit, and blood.

The enemy forces had begun to thin, the trucks they used for cover riddled with bullets. Seeing this Layla gestured an order to advance, then she charged the nearest truck, mowing down her armoured opponents with ease. Suddenly her rifle clicked dry so she tossed it drawing her knife only to be faced with three ominously armoured foes. Wasting no time she charged up to the closest man, grabbed his gun with her free hand and rammed her knife into his exposed neck under his helmet. The enemy shot her in the leg but it wasn't enough to stop her from pivoting and firing upon her assailant with her newly acquired gun. Panting in pain Layla saw a jet approaching in the distance just before her warehouse was hit directly with a bomb, sending her staggering face first into the parking lot. Light danced in her eyes as she awoke pain screaming through her whole body. The air now stunk of acrid burning cement. Moments later her vision cleared enough for her to see her pain wasn't just from her gunshot wound. She was being dragged by her legs towards a newly arrived hovertruck. She moaned in protest only for a staggering enemy soldier to limp over to her before kicking her violently in the side of her head.

Chapter 5 – The Leader's Rage

Icy cold water to the face blasted Layla awake. Struggling against fresh bounds Layla found herself tied to a broken metal light post. Her head and leg screamed in pain. Blinking away the pain, Layla found herself faced with multiple armed guards and a video camera that was filming her. A man with many metals pinned to his chest approached twirling a golden revolver in his hand. He pointed his revolver at her chest towards her many medals then he spoke in good English with a clear Chinese accent.

"We have captured one of your whore leaders. We have massacred your pathetic force of vagrants playing warrior. Now the West will watch what becomes of those who oppose Axis rule!" he growled. Layla stared at him defiant, unwilling to show her fear and sadness. She focused on thoughts of her family right until the revolver was pressed against her temple, and the trigger was pulled.

The Leader sat at his desk watching a live feed of the enemy's broadcast flanked by his children. All three were beyond enraged, barely able to restrain their tears.

"Who is he?!" The Leader boomed.

Revy gestured to the nearest Dust. "Sir, he's General Phillip Lee of the Chinese Communist Forces." The Dust said nervously. The Leader stood suddenly, seized the Dust by the throat and lifted her off the ground. "Why. Isn't He. Dead. Already?!"

"Sir... I'm certain the General is guarded at all times and we know his forces dwarf ours. Besides, wouldn't you rather end him yourself?" Revy asked, a hint of fear in her voice.

"Yes..." The Leader seethed, releasing the Dust whom bowed and scurried away.

"Revy, muster our forces. I want every Chinese and Russian living in Layla's glorious Canada to be killed." he growled.

"Even the civilians, sir?" Jonathan confirmed.

"Indeed. It's time someone takes back our country. While I breathe no outsiders will find salvation here."

Revy bowed. "With your leave, sir!" The Leader nodded so Revy sprinted to her mother's underground quarters where she finally allowed herself to burst into tears. Once she recovered Revy found herself looking at her mother's favourite dress laying abandoned on her bed. Resolute and enraged, Revy stripped down and donned the dress then strapped her favourite pistols to her bare thighs.

"I'll avenge you mother." Revy stated, smoothing the dress over her fit hourglass figure. Gathering herself, Revy rejoined her somber family.

"You look good my daughter." The Leader said with a hint of pride sneaking through his pain.

"Indeed." Jonathan concurred.

"Thanks. I'm off to go hunting."

"Take my best three Dust!" The Leader ordered.

"No need, father, I'm only going out a while to enact your whim. Not gonna take on the whole army myself."

"It wasn't a suggestion." The Leader boomed.

"Yes sir." Revy conceded, gesturing to a few nearby Dust and left via the elevator.

"What would you have me do, sir?" Jonathan asked straightening his tie.

"Your sister chose her path, given the circumstances... I grant you the same leave."

"Thank you, sir. In that case I'd like to join the army to avenge mother through her preferred official means."

The Leader teared up under his mask. "Don't die." he ordered.

"No worries, I'll join the civilian end under cover to aid in coordinating our response. Meanwhile, what would you like done with my position beside the Prime Minister?"

"A Dust is lined up to replace you to better help steer her response."

"Did you expect I'd want to move on?" Jonathan wondered.

"Yes, no son of mine would want to sit idly by. Go on your path."

"Thank you sir, what will you do, if I may ask?"

"My businesses came under attack doubtless because of the aid I provided the government, and the PM did next to nothing. It's time for new leadership." The Leader growled, his fists clenched.

Once Jonathan took his leave, the Leader gestured to his remaining Dust to set them loose, and left his mask behind then took the elevator up to his head-quarters. It was time for the enigmatic Rudolfo Aziz to bolster the people his own way.

I'd finished writing articles on the war when the news hit that General Layla Aziz had been assassinated on live TV. I found myself crying at the sheer horror of it all. George put his hand on my shoulder.

"Take the day, Murphy, go home, if your home's still there..." George said kindly.

"Thanks George." I said as I submitted my work and logged out. I walked through the city racked with fear as bombs continued to fall. Missiles rained down on maternity hospitals and residential areas with such frequency I genuinely didn't know if my home survived. On my way past the alley shortcut I'd been avoiding since encountering the Dust I heard a man scream. Against my better instincts I turned to see a Chinese soldier assaulting a civilian. I took a deep breath, yelled "Hey!", ran over and kicked him hard in his exposed balls as he stood to face me. I yelled for the man to run as I balled my fists ready to buy him time by getting my ass kicked. In the heat of the moment I forgot something obvious: soldiers have guns. He leveled his weapon at my face shouting something in Chinese. I closed my eyes expecting the end. I suddenly heard a loud bang and muffled thud. I opened my eyes to find the soldier dead before me, I turned to find a beautiful woman in a black dress with two silver pistols standing behind me.

"Th-thanks." I stuttered out aghast.

"No prob." she said then started walking away like nothing happened.

"Wait- I'm Murphy, Murphy Smith, who are you?"

"Rebecca. Call me Revy, it makes me happy."

Okay Revy, how do you feel about me calling the cops?"

She pointed a gun at me. "You threatening me Murph?"

I was shocked and afraid. "No, nope, no way... I'm grateful to you, I just meant we should report the body."

Revy burst out laughing. "Well aren't you naive, we're in the middle of a war, idiot. No one cares about one more Chinese body."

"Maybe you're right..." I conceded. Without so much as a goodbye she'd begun to walk away as though she was on a mission. I looked down the alley to confirm the man was gone and instead saw my neighborhood in ruins. I turned back to watch Revy walk away until I noticed some part of me felt unsafe without her so I found myself following her. Noticing me somehow she spun on her heel with gun at the ready.

"You wanna die, Murph?" she sneered.

I sighed. "No, I just don't have anywhere to go. I figured I'd be safest with you..." I admitted.

Revy harumphed then walked over to the soldier she killed. Wordlessly she tossed me his gun.

"There, now you're safe, goodbye Mr. Hero."

Unsatisfied, I kept following her.

Revy grumbled. "If it weren't for what you did I'd have shot you for annoying me so much."

"I saw what happened to General Aziz... I want to do more for Canada. Maybe you could teach me?" I asked.

Revy's eyes grew surprisingly sad. "Teach you what Murph?"

"How to survive...or something."

Revy suddenly grew angry. "You saw someone you don't even know die and you want to learn to fight? Are you an idiot or just not self aware? you're no fighter Murph!"

I was shocked. "What do you know about me? I just want to help!"

Revy holstered her guns and pinned me to a nearby wall. "You're just a journalist my... Master had to save. You're not cut out to be a killer. Walk away!"

"Master... wait, are they in charge of the Dust that saved me. Are they a Keeper? ... Are you?"

Revy covered my mouth with her hand. "Be silent lest I kill you, final friggin' warning! Follow if you want, but I ain't responsible if you die." she growled.

"Why would I die if you're here?" I said half-jokingly. I didn't comment on her slight blush.

"Journalists ask too many damn questions..." she grumbled.

I followed her downtown, trying to ignore her beating and shooting every Asian-looking person she found along the way, armoured or not. *I better stay quiet, or she might just shoot me.* I thought, trying my best to quell my queasy gut. *Why am I even following her? So what if she's a Keeper? At this point a secret society might be the only thing that survives this war...* Revy carefully and stealthily lead us to a building that sat alongside the skeletal remains of Aziz Solar Systems. Half of the building had collapsed, but Revy seemed unphased. I watched her place a hand against a brick wall and a camera hidden in a light post scanned her then the brick wall pulled into the building before parting into a doorway. Revy gestured that I follow which I nervously did into a cement stairway that lead down for what felt like kilometers. We walked down a long ornate hallway lined with medieval knight's armour until I realized I couldn't hear the sounds of war anymore. We bypassed a side hall, continuing down the hallway until we finally reached a massive rectangular space filled with darkness. I jumped when Revy clapped sharply to turn on the bays of florescent lights in the ceiling. Squinting in the sudden bright light, I took in the space: It was as big as a warehouse filled with people in suits with familiar masks all sparing with each other. There was also what looked like a basic elevator off to my right and a massive cherry wood desk that sat unmanned with monitors, documents, and an ancient-looking hourglass ticking down on it. Those warriors deep in their training all ceased with haste, turned to Revy and bowed.

"Dust, I bring you a fresh fleck of sand to refine. Spare him no wrath or face mine!" Revy ordered with a tone that shook me.

"Wait, what does that mean?" I asked.

"You gave up your chance to walk away, Fleck, now you'll become one with the Dust or you'll die. Good luck!" With that Revy walked back down the hallway. My mind was reeling. *It's all real?!* I thought. Before I could start blurting out questions a man in a black mask with a gold hourglass on its center approached me.

"I am Dust." he said coldly, bowed to me, then punched me square in the gut.

Doubling over in pain I coughed.

"Murphy Smith, how are you?" I choked out. In response he clocked me in the side of the head, sending me face first onto the cold cement floor.

"You are but a Fleck, not yet worthy to be Dust." he said coldly.

"Okay, I see how it is..." I groaned, putting my fists up in a boxer's stance. *Been a long time since my high school boxing days, hope I still got it!* I thought, loosing a jab his way which he dodged like his body was fluid. I kept up my attack to no avail until the Dust got bored of dodging then punched me in the gut repeatedly with insane speed before spin-kicking me directly in the head, knocking me out cold.

The Leader sat at home petting Rudy whom laid across his lap. Two phones sat on the coffee table in front of him. One was Rudolfo's and one was not. The other phone rang surprising him.

"Speak."

"Sir, the PM refuses to call an election despite the Deputy PM's willingness." the Dust explained.

The Leader looked at Rudolfo's phone. "I know, she told me." The Leader said.

"What would you have me do, sir?"

"It's time for new leadership. Your family will be compensated."

"Understood, goodbye."

The Dust assigned to the PM went to the bathroom then destroyed his phone thoroughly, flushing its SIM card. Taking a deep breath he reached into a secret compartment in his suitcase and pulled out a 3D printed knife. Years of deep cover would finally come to fruition. He knew his success meant death or life in prison, but would guarantee his place in the Leader's hourglass for eternity. Wasting no time, the Dust returned to the PM surrounded by officials and deeply slit her throat.

"Makenna what are you-oh my god!" A General exclaimed. The PM laid gurgling in a pool of her own blood, her body gasping for air. Wordlessly the Dust formerly known as James Makenna got down on his knees, closing his eyes as if in prayer. A nearby RCMP officer assigned to the PM's detail seized his hands and bound them.

"Why?!" the shocked General asked.

"Like sand through the hourglass, I am but Dust." the Dust said in response.

"You'll hang for this!" the RCMP officer growled, yanking him to his feet before hauling him away.

The Leader watched the news with a grim smile. The Prime Minister had been assassinated by a member of her cabinet. James Makenna had served his purpose. Now with the Deputy PM slated to call an election out of fear and a long-known sense of inadequacy it was truly time for Rudolfo to rise. He spent the day calling other business owners and his various Union head friends for potential endorsements of his fledgling campaign. With many commitments of support spurred on in part out of condolence for what happened to Layla, Rudolfo grabbed his mask and walked down to his spare office in the basement. It was time to rally the Dust.

One month of having my ass thoroughly kicked later and I was finally starting to hold my own. My Dust trainer rotated daily so I couldn't get comfortable. Not that thoughts of the war let me so much as sleep. But after a while I learned to rest as well as to fight. It was that or likely be killed based on Revy's statement. Every day I'd rise in the underground barracks, eat a nondescript military ration then be paired off with a Dust selected by Revy personally. I wasn't sure what her interest in me was of late, but I knew better than to spurn a potential connection. Without fail our people would rise, eat, bow to Revy, recite the pledge: "Like a sandstorm we will rage and envelope the world..." she'd begin.

"Blasting away the filth and reclaiming our birthright!" we'd finish. And then it'd be back to training. Not once in a whole month did anyone divulge their backgrounds, let alone their names. The most anyone would do was address me as a mere Fleck, unworthy to be Dust.

At first I was annoyed, but the sheer repetition seemed to wear me down until I stopped thinking about it at all, chalking it all up to the cost of safety in our current world. I'd yet to meet the true leader of this organization; I'd thought for a while it was Revy but one day she denied it before sicking another Dust on me. "You'll meet the Leader when he has use for you." was all Revy said before walking away, doubtless on another assassination run or something. If she came back at all it was always smelling of gunpowder and faint amounts of perfume. She didn't strike me as the perfume type, nor the dress wearing type, but every time I was lucky enough to see her she was clad in a fancy black dress that looked great on her regardless and one of those creepy Dust masks.

One day Revy returned following a massive man I'd never seen before. All of the Dust and Flecks ceased training immediately and bowed. Reading the room I bowed in turn.

"Flecks, this day I honour you with a purpose. But first pair off a fellow Fleck and spar. Winner becomes Dust. Begin!" The Leader boomed from behind his massive desk. I found myself facing off against a massive black man covered in tattoos. We fought for what felt like hours until I was sure my bones would snap from stress, but combining my training with my boxing experience earned me the upper hand. I stood over his dizzied face with my fist raised. Watching me, Revy started to clap then walked over, handing me a knife.

"Kill him, become my Dust." I took the knife, but the look in the Fleck's eyes stayed my hand as images of my previous life flowed through my mind's eye. I looked to Revy for resolve as I slowly brought the knife down.

"Stop!" The Leader boomed. Relief washed over me, stopping my hand from shaking with uncertainty.

"You, come here!" he ordered. I bowed to my opponent and jogged over to the desk with haste.

"I know my people, you I don't know... who are you?"

"I am but a Fleck, sir." I said reflexively.

"Not what I'm asking."

I stood there nervously for a second, "Murphy Smith, sir, a journalist."

"Ah, yes. What brings you to us Mr. Smith?"

"A Dust once saved me from Falco Jankins' assassins – I think that's who they were – then Revy saved me from my own weakness. She brought me here to train. I've been here over a month." I spouted out.

"Ah yes, I remember tasking the Dust to your aid, but Revy never mentioned her dealings with you. Tell me, Dust, if my daughter ordered you to kill, like recently, would you have done it?"

Part of me swelled with pride at being called Dust, despite barely knowing what the title entailed. "I'm not sure, sir. To be honest maybe, it'd just depend on the situation."

"The situation is she's ordered you to kill a person, nothing else matters. Your response?"

I was afraid to appear weak in front of the Leader, whom was also Revy's dad of all things, but I opted for honesty. "No sir, I'd need motivation of my own resolve..."

He suddenly stood, cutting an opposing figure. I could tell he was powerful in his own right despite his suit's efforts to restrain him. He offered me his hand to my shock. As we shook hands all he said was, "Good, I have enough murder-happy Dust, I could use someone with a little more tact, especially to help guide Revy."

Revy stormed over barely restrained, "I don't need or deserve a shackle... sir."

"Of course not love, but you do need someone in your life who doesn't shoot first and ask questions never."

I stood there awkwardly while the family of unknowns squabbled, afraid to interject. Revy blushed which spurred a sense of happiness in me I hadn't felt since high school. *She's deadly, but she can be cute too...* I thought.

"Yes, sir." she conceded, but I could see the frustration in her eyes.

The Leader turned to me. "I know your whole life, Smith, you're not just a desperate gutter rat who will kill for a suit, mask, purpose, and wage. I have use for your skill-set."

I was shocked when the Leader casually took off his mask to reveal enigmatic businessman and Prime Ministerial candidate Rudolfo Aziz of Aziz Solar Systems.

"No way!" I muttered despite myself.

"Indeed. Tell anyone and I'll kill you myself, clear?" he boomed. Everyone bowed immediately.

"But sir, you give solar energy to the poor and divest most of your holdings to fight homelessness. How do you also have time to run all of this?" I exploded.

None of it made sense. *How can a known family man and philanthropist also be head of an...assassin cult?!*

The Leader laughed, the jovial tone of which somehow immediately put me at ease.

"I've been doing this a long time, Dust. That's all I'll say. Now to your mission: I'll give you two million per year to be my campaign writer, expenses and housing included. In return you'll fall under Revy's command. What do you say?"

In that moment it hit me: *this man...this family... they had the late PM killed didn't they? Can I really work for people like that? I owe them both my life, and I'll probably be killed if I say no...so...* "What about my old job? George needs me." I worried.

"George's wife is one of us, he'll understand." The Leader revealed, his tone implying an 'or we'll kill him' caveat.

"Okay, then count me in, sir!" I exclaimed.

"Father, you can't be serious. I refuse to drag his useless ass around!" Revy whined in a way only the Leader's daughter could get away with.

"Let's see how useless he is then!" The Leader exclaimed, "Your knives and guns on the table now!"

Revy obeyed, getting the idea, and the Dust wisely cleared the floor for us.

"Mother trained me since I was old enough to walk, he can't win, Father." Revy's voice grew cold.

"I don't need him to win, I need him to impress you." The Leader explained.

"Fine, try!" Revy growled, striking at me like a coiled snake. Once more today I found myself desperately fighting for my life for what felt like hours. Except this time there was no way I could win.

"I'm. Sorry. For. What. Happened. To. Your. Mother. I. Wept. For. Her." I struggled out between blocking heavy blows. Revy blushed through her anger and faltered slightly, stopping just short of hitting me directly in the face.

"Your tears mean nothing to me!" she exclaimed, bowed to her father and marched off, guns in hand.

Chapter 6 – The Killer's Assistant

The Leader chuckled. "Yes, you'll do perfectly. I haven't seen her like that in years."

"Thank you, sir." I panted out, "With your leave, I need...rest."

Surprisingly he smiled gently, pushing a mask my way across his desk, "But of course you do, off you go. I have other recruits to test."

I went to bed satisfied, maybe even proud of myself. I was Dust now... Revy's Dust. I fell asleep thinking of her beautiful blushing visage and woke up sweating. I cleaned myself up, ate and donned a suit Revy had left on my cot with a note that simply said: "Dress proper from now on, Dust. Find me outside when you're awake." I ditched my old clothes, donned a bullet-resistant vest, and then the suit, which surprisingly fit perfectly. I patted the suit smooth until I felt something in my chest pocket. I pulled out a debit card in my name. I scanned the card with my bank app in my phone and my eyes went wide. I had over two million dollars. *The Leader wasn't kidding... holy crap. This is enough for a decent studio apartment.* I thought as I happily jogged past the elevator, back the way I came in. The brick wall-door closed behind me with just enough grinding noise I didn't hear Revy breathing in the shadows of the alley.

"You're finally awake, Dust. Good. Lots of Axis for us to hunt. Are you ready?" she asked.

"Yes Ma'am." I said, holding up my new mask. She tossed me a plastic bag full of weapons and donned her mask. "Let's go." she said seriously. Two other Dust joined us that dwarfed me, Revy's lieutenants.

I didn't know them as anything other than my teachers, but I respected them for it. My month of training couldn't prepare me for the death my team wrought on any armed person they could find. Part of me wondered if some of them were allies, but Revy seemed unperturbed. I drew my pistol to cover my allies so it'd look like I was doing something. I had to earn my apartment money somehow... though I couldn't stop thinking *I don't want to be a killer...* Yet for some reason, watching Revy headshot Axis units with ease excited me. *Am I a hypocrite? Being turned on by murder, but unwilling to pull the trigger?* I wondered. We walked until we came upon Paul's Diner, which we entered to clear out. Paul stood behind his counter, hands shaking as he tried to scrub a mug. We were surrounded by armed soldiers. Revy and the other Dust started firing without warning, the surprise of our attack greatly thinning their numbers before they could react. I watched the back door slam open. A huge armoured man stormed in, leveling his light machine gun on Revy who hadn't noticed over the sound of her pistols. I broke into a sweat, my body tensing. In that split second all I could think was *No!*

"Revy, down!" I yelled, opening fire. My full metal jacketed rounds slammed into the soldier's helmet, cracking his visor before brutally dispatching him. My murder virginity taken, fighting alongside my allies seemed easier. In no time Paul's Diner was a corpse house. I took in all the death, the stench, and my body once more broke into shakes. I almost threw up, but held it in. Then I noticed one of my teachers lying dead on the floor. I did my best not to cry in front of Revy, lest I get beat up for it or something. Instead she walked over and hugged me. The smell of her perfume relaxed me so in the safety of her arms I wept for the man I was.

Suddenly familiar sirens blared all around the diner. Cops streamed in wearing full riot gear, screaming for us to get down. I reflexively obeyed, but Revy just laughed at me.

"Like a sandstorm we will rage and envelope the world..." she said to the leader of the cops.

"Blasting away the filth and reclaiming our birthright!" the cops said, bowing to Revy.

Awkwardly, I stood, embarrassed by my civilian instincts. Revy handed the head cop a stack of money whom for his part just nodded before ordering his men to clean up the bodies. When they took my dead teacher away I looked to Revy.

"Shouldn't we bury him?" I asked sincerely.

She walked over to retrieve his mask for the next recruit, but it broke apart in her hand, too full of bullet holes. Her body language showed a sadness I knew she'd never admit to.

"No, his spirit has already become a grain in the Leader's hourglass." she explained.

"Understood." I said. *I don't get it, what will become of the bodies? Oh, whatever.* I thought.

Once the cops were gone I took of my mask and holstered my weapon then walked up to an overwhelmed Paul.

"You okay, boss?" I asked as gently as I could.

"F-fine... thanks. Drinks are on the house!"

"Huzzah, love you, Paul!" Revy exclaimed.

I joined her at the table with drinks in hand. Both of us took off our masks to drink. Revy's happy green eyes gleamed brighter than her grin which made my heart flutter. That was until her expression soured slightly. "What are you blushing for, Dust?" she demanded between sips.

"You're very beautiful... Ma'am." I stammered out honestly.

She started laughing so hard she almost choked. "You into me, or sumthin' Dust?"

"Yes Ma'am." I said seriously.

Revy downed two more mugs in silence. "Okay then, your honesty is appreciated. Drink up!"

Together we got good and drunk then marched back to the alley entrance uneventfully, as we were both oblivious to the ordinance still raining down on Toronto. We parted ways for the evening, her going to the female barracks while I took up my cot in the male side. I tossed my bullet-riddled suit aside and went to bed in my underwear hoping the pain in my core wouldn't keep me up. I practically blacked out until a sudden weight on my chest jarred me awake. I opened my sleep-filled eyes to find Revy on top of me, holding a finger up to her lips to silence me.

I blushed until my instincts got the better of me despite my urges. "No." I said.

"What do you mean no?!" she whispered angrily.

"We're drunk, it wouldn't be right..."

"Oh. My. God. Are you kidding? Murph, you killed for me... You! You say you want me now you say no?! Who cares if we're drunk?"

"I do!" I whispered seriously, my heart racing in anticipation of the very act I was stopping.

Revy's face was a wealth of emotions from anger, to annoyance, to frustration, and finally just a gentle smile.

"Fine. Forgive me, Dust." she whispered before kissing my forehead. I watched her slink away, cursing myself until I finally passed out again.

I awoke to find a new suit sitting on the floor beside me cot with a note that read "When you're ready. -R"

I picked up the suit and heard a metallic jingling sound. Inside the pocket was my debit card and a set of keys with an address label that pointed to the outskirts of the city. Like usual I put my bullet-resistant vest on first, suit next, and grabbed my mask which I stowed in my backpack for now. On my way out of the Leader's underground bunker I googled the address on the keys and set a waypoint on my phone. Part of me doubted hovercabs would still be running, but my luck prevailed. *Nothing stops a Toronto cabby eh?* I mused happily. We drove to the address to find a modest two storey bungalow sitting situated right by the road. I tipped the cabby handily then exited the cab. I wasn't sure what to expect, was this meant to be my new home? Upon ringing the doorbell I heard the low bark of a big dog, then Revy opened the door.

"Dust, welcome to my home, this is Rudy, he's harmless. Come, the Leader awaits you in the basement." I smiled at the big English Mastiff, amused by the idea that anyone in Revy's family could be harmless. Part of me wanted to address what happened last night but I opted to let the past be past, now it seemed it was time for business.

We marched downstairs with Rudy in tow to a simple yet heavy-looking metal door. Revy put one key in gesturing for me to use mine. "This key is a sign of trust, understand?" she said pointedly.

"Yes Ma'am." I said, turning my key in the heavy lock. Revy swung the door open to reveal one hell of a logistics center: it had a huge wooden desk with monitors, not unlike the underground base, cupboards filled with rations, work out equipment, a fully stocked gun rack, and even a dog bed for Rudy. The walls looked to be made of thick cement such that I doubted a direct missile strike would do much. The Leader pushed his monitors aside to reveal a disarming grin on his face. I smiled back, waiting for him to speak first.

"So you found the place, good!" he finally said.

"Yes sir, thank you for putting your faith in me." I said.

"After the lengths you went to for my daughter it was only natural. I knew you were special. Now, to business: You haven't seen me in a while because I've been busy campaigning with the write-ups you wrote for me in hand. Take a look."

Revy and I turned a monitor to see Rudolfo Aziz, Liberal was leading over his opponents by a mile in the polls.

"Seems the people love you, sir!" I exclaimed happily.

"Are you surprised? I'm not." Revy stated.

"No not at all, the amount of things Aziz Solar Systems does for this city his popularity was a sure thing." I admitted. *Not to mention how many homeless lives he's changed… less officially.* I thought, looking down at my suit.

"I need you to prepare me a victory speech with my promises to combat the economy, the war, homelessness and all that, clear?" he asked me.

"Yes sir!" I said.

"You're welcome to stay in the house, my son's room is free for the time being."

"Understood, thanks."

"Also, I'm not opposed to you two dating, just remember who's in charge at the end of the day."

Revy and I blushed but both managed to nod before heading upstairs.

"Did you tell him?" I whispered to Revy.

"Nah, he just knows stuff, got eyes everywhere ya know?" Revy grumbled.

"Seems you're used to this." I joked.

"You're not the first Dust I've taken as my own." she said in sultry way.

"I'm glad your father is so open-minded."

"He's always said life's too short, do what makes you happy, as long as it's legal."

I chortled. "Funny to hear he of all people cares about the law."

"Careful, Dust… but yes, I suppose it is quite funny these days."

Revy showed me to her brother's room, then took my hand, half-dragging me to her room.

Once we were done, I spent the remainder of my day writing speeches until I came up with something short and to the point:

Voters: You've put your faith in me for years to provide you with power, and now you entrust me with power of my own. Rest assured my every waking hour will be spent ensuring a better future for you and your loved ones. That means a more stable economy, a lowered housing market so you have safe places to live, an end to the war that has taken so many lives by any means necessary, a bolstering of our armed forces so we're never caught off-guard again, and last but not least, I'll work to eradicate homelessness to clean up our streets so when we rebuild we'll be better than before.

Chapter 7 – The Dawn of a New Age

I was at the Aziz family home in time to meet Jonathan, whom returned on leave from the army to support his father. Together we all watched the votes be cast. A camera crew was on site to film Rudolfo's beaming reaction as he won in a landslide victory with only forty percent of Canada having voted. Regardless for his first Prime Ministerial run, winning a majority was stellar. I was nervous when the army arrived to escort Rudolfo to his podium to give my speech, but he played it like a champ. The crowd loved him. Admittedly the opposition had made it too easy for team Aziz by being obsessed with cryptocurrency, and electing a creepy-looking leader who vowed to take women's reproductive rights away. Never mess with women, especially when they're the majority in numbers on the planet. I knew something voters only hoped was true: Rudolfo kept his promises; not only that he had 9000 Dust lined up to join the military should he win. During his speech, to my surprise, he opted not to live in the Prime Minister's house, instead opting to remain at his own. Though, thinking about it that basement of his would be an asset, especially with the scrutiny he'd now be under as PM.

I had no idea how he planned on handling the cost of housing, or the economy but the look on his face spoke volumes of his confidence. That evening after the RCMP had finished securing the house as best they could, I took Revy's hand and we met her father in his basement office. His hands were clasped in a business-like stance.

"Well, we did it." he said happily.

"You did it, sir." I corrected.

"Indeed, but now the real work begins."

"What would you have us do?" Revy asked seriously.

"Now that I'm PM you can't risk being seen on your Axis murder sprees. So, instead I'm appointing you both as my Ministers of Foreign Relations to Russia and China respectively."

I was shocked, "Sir, I'm just a journalist, I'm no politician. I'd be inept in that role."

"Shush, Dust." Revy ordered. The look in her eyes told me I wasn't thinking hard enough.

Rudolfo smiled. "Go easy on him, Revy, it's a day of celebration!" then he looked to me, "I don't need you to be a politician. I'm sending you both into those viper's nests so we're ready when diplomacy...gets difficult." My eyes went wide, Revy smiled coldly.

"Sir, you lost your wife to this world, would you truly like to risk your daughter on the off chance she can't make it home?" I asked carefully.

Rudolfo's muscles bulged but he calmed himself. "You are both Dust, for the betterment of the world I can and will ask anything of you. It may come to pass that your...specific services aren't required, but should they be I would have you remain resolute." he said seriously.

He means it too. Sacrifice me, fine, but Revy?! I thought. *I can't let anything happen to her!*

"Like a sandstorm we will rage and envelope the world..." Rudolfo boomed.

"Blasting away the filth and reclaiming our birthright!" we finished.

"As we speak almost all of my 9000 local Dust have embraced their civilian selves to join the army. Meanwhile I have recruiters combing the homeless population that remains with offers greater than MC execs can counter; this should ensure a fresh stream of trainees and less lifespan for the useless execs."

"Two birds, one stone: Lower the homeless population and raise an army at the same time." I was impressed by the efficiency of the idea.

"I'm glad you approve," the Leader said eyeing my smile, "In regards to the economy, America of old proved the best way to a strong economy is through a strong army. What Canada lacks, we'll re-appropriate from the Axis countries. Once our Military Industrial Complex is booming I'll have the money to re-build Aziz Solar Systems and housing will soon follow. Housing is my last concern as I'll have lots of room in the barracks for our beloved homeless population to magically disappear into. And after war time we'll have lots of freshly leveled land to rebuild on courtesy of our Axis 'friends.'"

I was mildly shocked at how clearly he'd laid all that out, but it made sense, he'd been running a shadow organization with international reach presumably for decades, what's running a country by comparison? Our marching orders in hand, we returned upstairs waiting for the military escort to the PM's cabinet reveal. I sat side by side with Revy, flanked by armed guards. The Leader was in a separate truck for safety.

"Are you sure about this? Us being... Ministers during this war?" I asked Revy carefully.

"Of course I'm sure, I've been waiting for a job this big my whole life. You ain't pussin' out on me are ya, Murph?" she said, catching my true meaning. I was flabbergasted. *How does one inspire such loyalty in a world like this?* I thought, keeping my resolve as high as I could. *I hope the war ends without us having to be political assassins... at least for Revy's sake, she's all I have to live for.* I almost found myself wishing I was still a lonely, broke journalist. Almost.

I thought back to the day I broke the Falco James story and how afraid of retaliation I was then, that paled in comparison to how afraid I was now: standing shoulder to shoulder with a cabal of Union reps and randoms the Leader picked for his cabinet. It was a diverse bunch, but I couldn't shake the feeling we were seconds away from being bombed into oblivion. However in our nondescript ice hockey rink no bombs fell. Hands were shook, titles exchanged, then we mercifully went home. I still felt the searing judgment in the eyes of my fellow cabinet members. Thankfully none of that mattered since my appointment to the position was superficial at best. I didn't expect to have to do much of anything until the day would come for me to pick up a 3D printed knife. Revy just beamed the whole time like she was a kid in a candy store, oblivious to the judgment of our peers or the fear I felt. I often got the sense she'd just shoot a bomb out of the sky if she had to.

Revy and I spent our final night together knowing full well we'd be shipped off tomorrow. She got assigned to China while I got Russia. The Leader instructed us to leave our weapons behind so the next day we parted maybe for the final time. I was full of fear, but less so for me. No, I was afraid for Revy. She was way too excited to go on this suicide mission. The Leader implied the night before that resources would be there for us, but didn't elaborate. Thinking about him frustrated me. How could he risk his only daughter like this? Was it confidence or coldness that drove him? During our time together I'd begged Revy to find an undetectable poison to use so that maybe she'd have a chance to escape. She just smiled at me gently, saying nothing. On the way to the airport I read up on my target via a dossier the Leader provided. Russia's dictator changed names often, moved locations even more often, and only showed up for very public appearances staying inside a sniper-proof see-through box when outside. There was no way I'd have an easy time getting to him. Naturally, world leaders had bolstered their security following the previous PM's assassination. On one hand I was somewhat relieved as it meant no face-to-face risk for me, but on the other hand I had zero clue what to do beyond pretend to be a good Minister. All I knew was this bastard had amassed hundreds of years of life by exploiting babies and the homeless, no different than the MiraiCorp bastards I'd gotten fired.

My flight to Russia went off without a hitch leaving me standing at what I thought was the Receiving terminal. Awkwardly, I roamed around looking for a person holding a sign with my name on it. What I eventually found was a familiar face: the Dust that I'd spared during my final initiation fight. He was a big black man with an equally big smile. He wore an RCMP uniform.

"Hello there." I said happily.

"Greetings Mr. Smith. I'm happy to say I'll be your guard for the remainder of your trip! Name's Devante Jones" he explained.

"Glad to have you Mr. Jones, shall we?"

"Yes, we have much to discuss."

Adopting a brisk march, he led me to an armoured hover-SUV with a Canadian Flag adorning its antennae. Once inside he turned serious.

"I owe you my life." he stated.

"No worries, so, you're a Mounty huh?"

"Yessir, born and raised. Dad was a Mounty too."

"What brought you to the Leader?"

"I fell on hard times after I was laid off due to injury. The Leader found me in the gutter and gave me new life, literally. You?"

"Revy saved me and brought me in." I said trying to suppress my worry.

Noticing my expression he smiled, "She'll be fine, the Leader wouldn't have chose her if he wasn't certain of that."

"I hope so."

"She'll have guards like you do, sir."

"So, the Leader promised me resources..."

"Indeed, you get me, a few other Mounties, and this:" he said, handing me a suitcase. Inside of its secret compartment was a mask, a loaded silenced pistol, a vial of some unknown clear substance, a burner phone, and my clearance papers.

"I'm guessing this vial is poison?" I asked hopefully.

"Yessir, it's fast acting and fat-soluble, leaves no trace."

Good so Revy will have the same I'm sure...she better use it. I thought, somewhat relieved.

Devante drove us to our hotel where we met with Russian delegates and got to work. Thankfully my Mounty ally spoke some Russian and the Russians brought an interpreter. Their leader was nowhere to be seen.

Prime Minister Rudolfo Aziz sat at his desk with Rudy by his side, having video chats with Canada's allies.

"Rudolfo, as I said before we can't commit any troops to your aid, the Axis are threatening to nuke us if we do. We aren't equipped to respond!" The British PM said.

"And what do you think will happen if they get all of Canada's resources, they'll just bend over and leave you alone?!" Rudolfo boomed, a hint of the Leader's impatience coming out in his tone.

"I'm sorry, our hands are tied. Even without the threat of nukes we just don't have any troops."

Frustrated, Rudolfo hung up on his supposed allies, "Of course not, because they wasted their lives believing in you!" he growled.

I hope the Dust is fairing better than I am. He thought, looking at a picture of Revy on his desk. Wringing his hands to counter stress build-up, Rudolfo flipped his ornate golden hourglass once more.

Revy sat in her Chinese hotel with her Mounty escort close by. She juggled her silenced pistol from hand to hand, spinning it like a cowgirl until even she couldn't ignore the nervous looks on her escorts' faces. Giggling to herself, Revy stowed the pistol in her suitcase for later, picking up the vial of poison her father had provided her.

"So to be clear this isn't for me, right?" she joked.

"No ma'am. It's for your target ideally." one Mounty said seriously.

"I'm kidding, dumbass. Based on my recon and this dossier the target likes to be in the open. Easy sniper target. Shame all I have is this piddly little pistol..."

"Yes, she's very cocky. Rumour has it she believes all of the lifespan she's amassed makes her un-killable."

"What an idiot, she should kill whoever convinced her of that. But it makes my job easy so I guess I should thank them."

"Ma'am, a thought if you'll permit me..." The Mounty said nervously.

"Go ahead."

"Allow me to take over this mission. It'd be much easier to dismiss me as a rogue agent than the Leader's daughter should I get caught."

Revy pointed her gun at the Mounty, "You doubt me, Dust?!" she seethed.

"No Ma'am, it's just my primary mission is your safety!" the Mounty cowered.

"Pfff. Who cares, end of the day I'm just Dust like you. The Leader just trusts me more, that's all. Don't bring this up again!" Revy grumbled.

"Yes Ma'am, with your leave then, the conference is about to start."

I followed Devante and our interpreter to the world leader's conference being held over live stream. It was uneventful, every one of our supposed allies had capitulated to the Axis forces' nuke threats. The justification being that the supposed immortality of the Chinese dictator meant she really wouldn't mind billions dying as long as she genuinely believed her family would survive. On the Russian end of things their dictator believed too highly in his security and anti-missile systems, but did not have the sense to condemn his ally's mad immortality idea. I knew all too well thanks to Falco James that it didn't matter how good a ninja one was, nor how much life they'd accrued, a well placed bullet would always mean death. I typed out my notes for the Leader whom wasn't in attendance then lead Devante back to our room. *Looks like the only way forward ends in death.* I thought dejectedly.

When we got back to our room I felt my suitcase vibrate. I pulled out the burner phone right in time to answer it.

"Sir?" I said.

"Report." the Leader said.

"It seems as long as current leadership holds among the Axis powers, nuclear war is all but assured. Worse still, no one is willing to help us..."

"That's what I'm getting on my end too. Are you prepared to do your duty?"

"Yes sir, but I have no way of getting anywhere near my target."

"I figured as much. Time for a career change. How do you feel about being a room service valet?"

"Understood, I'm to dose his food."

"Correct though your face is known. I'll have a local Dust take the food to him, you need only sneak into the kitchens and plant the poison. The Dust will be sent a picture of your face, he knows the mask."

"Consider it done sir." I said. He hung up, so following protocol I destroyed the phone and flushed the SIM card.

I turned to Devante, "Ready for some spy stuff?" I asked.

"Oh yes!" he said smiling.

"Remember: No English." I warned.

I tossed Devante my gun so he could cover me, we changed suits to be less conspicuous, put on our masks in case there were cameras, and headed down the elevator to the kitchens. It was midnight by the time the elevator stopped but the floor was alive with people. My heart raced in my chest. I double-checked that the vial was in my pocket then Devante and I tailed a dish boy as casually as possible into the kitchens. I nodded to Devante and the big black man pistol whipped the dish boy and I stuffed him in a corner. All told the kitchen was a skeleton crew to my delight. There were two chefs and cleaning staff, but nothing we couldn't handle.

I grabbed a chef's knife off of the counter then motioned for Devante to do the same. *Gun will be too loud.* I thought, he seemed to understand. We waited crouched behind a counter until the cleaning staff went into another room, then I grabbed a chef from behind and pressed my knife to his throat, Devante followed suit with the other chef.

"President's food, where?" Devante asked in Russian. Both chefs pointed to a covered dish. I choked out my chef carefully while Devante slit his chef's throat. I gave him a dirty look under my mask. *There goes our no kill bonus score.* I thought to myself. Quickly I emptied the vial into the dish, loaded it onto a trolley and we rushed into the hallway. I nearly ran into a valet who took one look at me and bowed. "Dust" was all he said, but it was enough for me. I handed over the trolley then we piled into the elevator. Just as the elevator doors closed I heard screaming. I could still smell the iron in the chef's blood over the delicious smells of cooked food. Our Dust ally bowed to me as we got off on our floor and he continued up to the executive suites to finish the job. Quickly we hid our masks, but there was no one awake to see us.

Once we were back in our room, I hugged Devante whom was caught by surprise. Awkwardly we parted, then he pulled out his own burner phone to report in.

After he hung up he gave me a small smile.

"The Leader sends his congratulations. The local Dust just confirmed food delivery. There's a plane waiting for us at the airport now."

"We better hurry, the police might lock this place down any moment now!" I exclaimed, stowing my mask, my knife, and the empty vial in my suitcase's compartment with my destroyed phone. We changed into street clothes and strolled out of the hotel just as sirens could be heard in the distance. I was elated, Devante practically whooped for joy. Quickly I hailed us a hovercab then we took a long ride to the airport. My credentials from the beginning of the mission got us past bag check without issue, we boarded the private flight, and flew back to Canada with one less "President" to worry about.

Chapter 8 – Revy

Revy destroyed her burner phone having received her orders.

"Team Russia succeeded, now it's all us. You ready?" Revy asked.

"Yes Ma'am" the Mounty said, loading her gun. Revy didn't care to ask the Mounty's name, they were just Dust to her. What she did care about was not being upstaged by Murphy Smith of all people. Revy donned one of her mother's dresses while the Mounty changed into a dinner suit. They checked out of the hotel, carrying their bags with them in an optimistic bid to leave quickly once the deed was done.

Revy's silenced pistol was holstered to her leg under a slit in her dress while her mask was folded away into her cleavage. The vial of poison was sequestered in a small pocket in her dress that wasn't big enough for the mask. Revy hailed a hovercab which took them right to the venue where the Chinese President was slated to give a speech. Having flashed her credentials at the door, Revy and the Mounty followed their interpreter to a gallery with a podium. To Revy's delight there was exposed water glasses on the podium in a cubby under the mic, but the room was packed with people all watching the podium from military to eager civilians. *Sorry Murph, looks like I gotta do this guns blazing. That's more my style anyway.* Revy thought, a small grin forming on her face.

One nod to the Mounty and a vague gesture to the holster spoke volumes about the direction the night was to take. The Mounty nodded grimly. Both women checked their holsters carefully then waited for the President to arrive. Moments later the President marched down the hallway up to the podium, the lights in the venue dimmed leaving only a spotlight on Revy's target. *Too easy!* Revy thought happily. She allowed the President a moment to speak to put the room at ease then both women drew their guns. One barely silenced bang cut the President's speech short abruptly. The whole room watched as her body dropped like a log, a pool of blood spilling onto the floor. In that moment chaos erupted. Revy donned her mask then very casually began walking into the fleeing crowd. Some military members attempted to stop her only to be shot by the Mounty.

"I've got this, go!" The Mounty yelled. Revy waved in response, walking away. Under her mask the Mounty blushed. *I always had a thing for you, Revy, but even though I fought for this posting you'll never even know my name. Oh, whatever, just survive love.* Revy stowed her mask in her dress as she followed the crowd out of the building. Behind her the sound of silenced gunshots abated or were drowned out by screams, Revy couldn't tell. She strode into a nearby bathroom, ripped off her outer dress, then used a lighter to light the dress and mask on fire underneath a smoke alarm.

Goodbye, Dust. Thank you. She thought. Before Revy could react, Chinese military hover-trucks surrounded the building. Keeping her cool, Revy prepared to flash her credentials, but didn't notice one of the army commanders had a laptop. On the screen was security camera footage of her putting on the mask and shooting the President.

"Halt!" the commander said to her in perfect English.

Revy froze, her free hand drifting down to her holster. "I'm Minister of Foreign Affairs to China, Rebecca Aziz, let me pass!" Revy ordered.

"We know who you are!" The commander gestured sending his men to surround Revy, guns at the ready. *Damn, I'm blown!* Revy thought. Smiling ruefully she stood calmly while the soldiers bristled around her.

Suddenly a hover-limo honked and pushed through the shocked soldiers.

"I'm Dust, get in!" the driver yelled.

Thanks Daddy. Revy thought as she dove in the vehicle and the driver took off. Military units gave chase but the driver was smart, taking shortcuts until they had traffic in between them. It helped that civilians had fled the theater in droves following the fire alarm. Thereby holding most of the soldiers up. Once they were in the clear the pair switched vehicles by hijacking an empty hover-cab.

"Thanks, Dust, I owe you one!" Revy exclaimed happily.

"I'm no Dust, I'm a Dagger..." he growled as he drew a pistol. With practiced grace Revy drew her pistol and both shot at the same time. Revy and the driver died instantly. When the cab company GPS tracked their car the bodies were found. On the Dagger they found a familiar mask, one that matched the security footage from the hotel. The Leader's best Dust had been tricked and swept away in one brutal moment.

Proudly, I rang the doorbell to Revy's home. Devante had opted to leave for his own place when we landed, which was fine by me. I was looking forward to some celebratory alone time with Revy. To my surprise Jonathan opened the door with a look of grim sadness etched all over his face.

"The Leader awaits, let's go." he said gesturing for me to enter. We marched down to the locked basement door, put in our respective keys and entered the dark space.

I was shocked to find the Leader cradling Rudy with tears streaming down his face.

"Congratulations on your success, Dust... Canada and the world owe you a great debt..."

"Thank you sir. Why are you crying?" I asked, filled with discomforting confusion.

"It's my sincerest regret to inform you that Rebecca has been killed."

"What, how?!" I blurted out.

Jonathan put his hand on my shoulder in a comforting gesture that I also took as a warning to calm myself.

"After accomplishing her mission she was brutally murdered by unknown forces outside the venue." the Leader explained.

I couldn't believe my ears. I thought for certain this was some cruel test. How could I, a novice Dust, have outlived my teacher whom had far more experience than me?

"I... I'm sorry sir, it should've been me." I stammered out as tears streamed down my cheeks.

"No! It should've been me, or barring that if you suddenly felt sentimental, it should've been one of your many Chinese Dust... not Revy... dear sister!" Jonathan seethed.

"Enough!" The Leader boomed. Rudy jumped up and ran to his bed. "You think I don't have regrets, boy?! First your mother, now Revy, this war takes its toll. Rest assured had I any doubt in my heart I would've sent a Dust, but I underestimated the damned Chinese. Never again!"

Jonathan recoiled at his father's outburst of rage then broke down into tears himself. The Leader walked over to embrace his only remaining child, leaving me to feel like a voyeuristic third wheel.

After a while they parted with the Leader returning to his desk. "Dust, when you check your account you'll find a sizable reward has been transferred. Enjoy. Also be aware that your cover is blown. As of this moment, consider yourself Prime Ministerially pardoned, but that will take time. So stay low for a while."

"Understood, thank you, sir. If I may ask, what's next?" I asked, wiping tears from my eyes.

"Dust-backed riots are taking place in both countries as their beheaded governments scramble to nominate replacements. I already have Dust inserted into government roles with hopes that they'll take over, but I can't contact them now that transmissions to and from Canada are being monitored. In short, scrutiny has befallen me, but things will work out, in this lifetime, or the next."

"Understood sir, I have all faith in our Dust to ensure success." I said with certainty.

"Take heart that Revy's death wasn't in vain. You two may've just averted nuclear war!" The Leader said with a hint of tearful pride.

"What would you have me do?" Jonathan asked.

"Leave the army and move back home. I can't bear to lose another family member! And bring that army boyfriend of yours, I'd like to meet him!"

"How'd you know?!" Jonathan blushed.

"I always know." The Leader said gently

Jonathan and I left the basement preparing to head our separate ways.

"Are you mad at how things turned out?" I asked him.

"More distraught than anything. I wish it had've been me." he said sadly.

"I find comfort in the fact Revy fought for this mission. She would've been proud of herself no doubt."

"I just don't understand why I wasn't sent. I've always been the black sheep of the family..."

"May I ask why?"

"I was born Joanna. Took many years and much convincing from mother for father to even allow my transition. I would've thought part of him would relish in sending me on some suicide mission..."

"I couldn't tell, you're a man to me, and I'm sure he doesn't think that low of you. Even if he does that's his problem, you're you, not whoever you were born as in the beginning." I said seriously.

"Thanks Murphy." Jonathan said, shaking my hand, "I just wish Revy were okay. She always supported me. Hell, she once shot a guy who called me a girl." Jonathan said, smiling wistfully.

"That sounds like Revy..." I laughed. With that we parted ways, Jonathan was off to get discharged from the army, while I headed to my nice studio apartment I'd acquired before leaving for my suicide mission. On the hover-cab ride home I checked my bank balance. *Holy shizz, another four million? I'm rich!* I thought laughing to myself, knowing full well I'd be lucky to get a small house for thirty million. Regardless I was more than well off enough to own a big TV, which I turned on when I got home.

I was a little shocked to find mine and Revy's faces plastered all over the news. We were being called assassins and Rudolfo Aziz was indeed under scrutiny as the news reported the UN was looking into his dealings. I was amazed at the speed of which the news had been gathered. They even had a picture of our mask. Questions were reportedly being raised as to the origin of the mask as security cams had indeed picked up both our teams wearing them. On that point I wasn't worried, no Dust would ever betray the significance of our mask, especially not now that rioters were reportedly wearing knock-offs of them as a symbol of freedom. In other good news, I tuned into the UN meeting on Rudolfo to find all of Canada's allies had immediately voted for his innocence. "I guess they aren't completely useless after all!" I muttered happily. The vote ended inconclusively so investigations were doubtless still ongoing, but at least further war wasn't being declared on us. Air raid sirens still pierced the night since Axis ordinance was still being dropped on us; despite our best efforts the war was still ongoing. Much of Canada was without power or running water. People prostituted themselves openly in the rubble-filled streets, desperate to afford even a bottle of water. The news reported that women were writing their bank info on their kids' backs so relatives could take care of them should their mothers die in the war. The state of Canada was one of abject misery, yet here I was, comfortable and relatively safe. *After all I've done, morally it doesn't seem fair.* I mused, staring down at my mask which I removed from my pocket. Devante had done me the favour of disposing of my suitcase, not that it mattered since the world seemed to know or think I was a killer anyway. If the Leader's pardon did come through it likely wouldn't help my public image any, but I didn't care. I turned off my TV, crawled into bed, and dreamed of Revy's smiling face.

Chapter 9 – Pardoned but not Forgotten

I awoke to find my official pardon in the mail. Elated, I turned on the TV to find the Leader under attack for pardoning myself, Revy, and our Mounty partners so quickly. I resolved to thank him next time we met then headed to Best Buy to get myself a new gaming PC in celebration. When people saw me some jeered, but most, to my shock, broke into cheers. "Hero!" some called me, "Murderer!" fewer still called me. I supposed in a way both were true, but the former was a matter of interpretation at best. The war hadn't ended, so I didn't feel too heroic. I brought my PC home then decided to go for a walk; that was a mistake.

"It's you!" a voice shouted from behind me. I turned to see four men with knives surrounding me. The speaker had a strong Russian accent.

"The KGB sends regards from the late President's family!" he said.

I sighed, "Look, I get it, but can we not and say we did? It's been a day." I groaned.

"No... we can't." the speaker, a big man said. His friends were no slouches either. Wordlessly I focused on dodging as fluidly as my teachers were, not keen on being offensive with just my fists. My opponents were clearly trained well. I struggled to avoid getting cut. The only advantage I had was that I'd kept my bullet-resistant vest on under my suit out of paranoia. Beginning to get frustrated, I punched a guy in the wrist hard enough that I could smoothly take his knife. With the hard part over, I swung deftly slitting the owner's wrist with it. Now it was only a matter of time before it was three on one. Not to be outdone, his allies struck fast and hard, going for my legs, my tendons, anything they thought was exposed. I kept dodging as best I could but my suit was in tatters.

Suddenly a hover-car pulled up. Expecting more enemies I sighed, but instead shots rang out above the din of distant explosions. My enemies dropped like logs.

"Miss me?" Devante said joyfully from behind the wheel.

"Hell yes brother, what are you even doing by my place?"

"My mom made spare casserole, said I should deliver some to my friends, and well, you're the closest thing I have to a friend. So yeah!" he explained.

Ha! I got saved by casserole?! Revy would die laughing. "Thanks man, come on over, my place is this way."

I hopped in Devante's ride and guided him to the parking area. We went inside to eat.

"So, we even now?" he asked over a mouthful of food.

"Damn straight!" I exclaimed. His eyes beamed with happiness.

"So, where's your family?" he asked.

"No family, parents passed of lung cancer cuz we couldn't afford the medical bills, and me... I'm forever alone cuz no woman wants to bother with a poor journalist... even less so with a government assassin." I whined.

Devante just laughed. "Nah, you're one of the good ones. When you've finished mourning Revy hit me up, my sister's forever single too!"

"What about you, your family good?"

"Ya brother, mom's fresh outta hospital for a hip replacement paid for by yours truly. Blessed be the Leader. Sister's a homebody, but she's good. Other than that I've just been laying low avoiding people."

"Ya, based on today I think I'll move into the Barracks or the Leader's place. I'm too much a target as of late." I admitted.

"Choose the Leader's place man. He needs guards now more than ever, and if you're being tailed by Axis goons, we can't risk the barracks being discovered."

"True enough. I hope he's alright." I conceded.

"I'll help you pack then we'll go see the Leader together!" Devante said.

Rudolfo Aziz sat alone at his second command desk in the basement of his family home being interrogated by world leaders.

"You recently finalized a deal to purchase MiraiCorp and all of its holdings outright, and now stand accused of financing coups in China and Russia. Are you trying to control our livelihoods?" A Minister asked.

Yes. "Of course not minister, my aim was to clear out the rampant corruption in MC, as for the recent assassinations I take no responsibility. Has any evidence arisen to implicate me?" Rudolfo asked gently.

"Not as of yet though the KGB claims to have transcripts of calls between the assassins and their leader, obtained by auditing cell towers in the area."

This is why I change my voice when speaking to Dust. "You won't find anything to implicate me in those."

"So it's merely coincidence the calls originated from a cell tower in your area?"

No. "Of course it is, anyone can bounce calls off of different towers these days. At worst this is a shoddy frame job."

"And I'm sure it's coincidence your daughter, a well as her mysteriously appointed Minister boyfriend, Murphy Smith, got caught on CCTV moments before the murders wearing these?" The Minister pulled up an image of Revy's bloodied mask.

No. "Yes, that's just an easily obtained Halloween mask with what looks like an hourglass painted on it. Who knows what that means..."

"You do, Prime Minister, your daughter died having this very mask. You can't tell me you knew nothing!"

Don't remind me. "I did not and would not send my own daughter to play assassin with no hope of ever returning."

"Plausible, but what of this Murphy Smith, was his mother also assaulted by a Russian?" The Minister asked pointedly.

"I barely know Mr. Smith. I was introduced to him only recently by my daughter. I don't police her boyfriends. Mr. Smith was employed on contract with my organization to use his journalistic skills to write a successful Prime Ministerial campaign. As far as I know he had no connections to Russia."

"But you did wire him over six million dollars via Aziz Solar Holdings did you not? Why?"

"As payment for using his journalistic skills to write my successful Prime Ministerial campaign." *The best lies have grains of truth...*

"Then why am I just getting word that KGB agents sent to intercept Mr. Smith never called in?"

"I don't know." *Truth...for once.*

"I think you do. And I think you're using shell companies to pay people like the Mounties sent as your "Ministers'" detail."

"Can you prove any of this or are you just eager to be sued for besmirching my good name and that of my colleagues?" Rudolfo asked pointedly.

"No I can't, but I will remind you that even you cannot sue a UN minister."

"Isn't that lucky for you?" Rudolfo remained polite, but wanted to growl out that last line.

"We'll be in touch, Prime Minister." with that the video conference ended. Rudolfo let out a sigh of relief. *The phones are a dead end, my Dust techs assured me of that, but what's this about Smith and the KGB?* Rudolfo thought. Just then the doorbell rang.

I rang the doorbell at the Leader's house and surprisingly he answered, came outside, and closed the door.

"Sir." I said.

"Dust." he acknowledged. "I'll make this quick as my house may be bugged by now. How would you feel about a holiday to Italy?"

"I wouldn't mind that at all, though Devante here convinced me you may need me around as a guard."

"I don't, I'll have Jonathan. I'm assigning you to bolster our forces in Italy. The Keeper Leader there is one Jonas Valenti, he'll take over command from me until this war and the scrutiny that comes with it, blows over."

"I thought you were the worldwide Leader sir?"

"Negative, I just have connections with every country's Leader. Leading the whole world solo is too big a job for one man, even if clandestine ops are often very similar in structure. Technically I am the Keeper Above All, but I don't rub it in."

"Understood, and how am I to bolster Sir Valenti's forces once I'm there?"

"The same way Revy recruited you. These days every country has no shortage of homeless and destitute just looking for money and purpose. Use them. Feel free to take this Dust with you." he said pointing to Devante. "Dismissed." We nodded instead of bowing in case people were watching then hopped in Devante's car headed for the airport. It sucked to abandon my new gaming PC at home so soon, but I hoped Italy would offer respite from my Russian enemies, and really found myself hoping the Leader would somehow wrap up this war so I'd still have a home to go back to.

The airport loomed ahead. "Thanks for the ride, Devante, but I'm going on this adventure alone." I said.

"You sure?" he asked.

"Yes, your family may be targets now that our faces are out there, they need you more than I do."

"Okay brother, good luck, train up lots of Dust!"

"You bet!" I shook his hand, grabbed my travel bag and took off on my flight to Italy.

At the receiving terminal a man in a purple suit with a red lapel held up a sign with my name.

I approached him cautiously. "Like a sandstorm we will rage and envelope the world..." I started

"Blasting away the filth and reclaiming our birthright!" he finished. *I'm glad the mantra is consistent around these parts and he speaks English too. Good.* I thought, shaking the man's hand.

"I am but Dust." he said.

"As am I, though you're dressed quite flamboyantly for Dust." I joked.

"You chide me for standing out when you and yours brought our mask into the public light?"

"Fair play." I conceded.

"Come, I'm to take you to our Leader."

The Dust drove us to an underground parking center somewhere in the city. He placed his hand on the brick wall. A nearby camera turned our way, then the bricks receded into an opening not unlike the alley entrance in Toronto. We walked past empty barracks after empty barracks until we were finally faced with a room full of Dust. I reached into my suitcase for my mask, but my new friend stayed my hand. "No need here." he said. I reflexively turned ready to fight when I heard a loud thump on a nearby wooden table. The sound triggered the overhead lights revealing an older gentleman in a dinner suit with a mustache and goatee.

"Mr. Smith, you've graced us with your presence at long last!" the gentleman said politely.

My driver bowed so I bowed in turn, "Leader?" I asked carefully.

"Indeed. Am I what you were expecting? Speak freely." he said.

"If I'm honest I was expecting a younger, beefier man." I admitted.

The Leader laughed. "Ah yes, but of course, you serve Master Rudolfo, the Keeper Above All. So you think us all alike, no?"

I nodded yes.

"I prefer my experience to show on my face, while others prefer the raw muscle of youth. But enough about me, let's talk about you. A journalist turned assassin for love whom helped take down the Russian President. An impressive resume to say the least."

"Thank you sir. I was told I'm here to recruit and train Dust?"

"Not so, you're here, I'm afraid, to be bait for the True Knights of Artorious..."

"You've lost me, sir. I thought the Keepers and their Dust were the true Knights of Artorious?"

"Oh, but we are. They're a rival faction set up within the last 100 years by an unknown party. They claim to be the true inheritors of the wealth of the Knights Templar. Thus they believe themselves superior to our 'meager' efforts."

"So they're Knights Hospitaller wannabes. If I may be so bold, what does this have to do with me?"

He smiled. "So you know your history, good. It involves you because these wannabes as you put it were enraged by yours and Miss Aziz' actions of late. Our sources within the 'order' indicate the dictators you slew were their puppets."

"So they blame us, well with Revy gone, they blame me... great." I sighed.

"I'm told Master Rudolfo is attempting to install our own agents in those recently vacated positions, but that will take time, time I'm afraid we may not have."

I shrugged. "Why would the Keepers have reason to fear a relative upstart if our info is correct?"

"Never underestimate the underdog, Dust. You were but a journalist mere months ago, look at you now."

"Fair..." I said.

"Rumour has it the wannabes are the ones behind the nuclear weapons threats. If they aren't dealt with your work will have been for naught."

"Jesus…" I muttered.

"Do not speak the Lord's name in vain." he scolded. I bowed in apology.

"Forgive me, Leader. What are my orders?" I asked.

He smiled. "Go out, enjoy the scenery, be a tourist! Your face paints a target on you big enough to be seen from space; doubtless you'll bring our enemy out of the shadows. Meanwhile, take comfort in knowing my entire Dust unit will be out there with you with blades at the ready, just less conspicuously than yourself."

I bowed to the Leader, bowed to the Dust who'd be my guardians and left the way I came in.

For days I wandered through Italy like the lost tourist I was. Eventually I gave up trying to speak Italian, opting to play off my presumed ignorance for what it was worth. Whenever In got lost I'd just say I was Canadian and magically people became more helpful. I bounced from restaurant to restaurant, blowing my converted millions on luxury foods like I was slated to die the next day. However I was careful not to over-eat lest I was ambushed by Italian assassins…or counter-assassins, whatever they were. Little did I know then how glad I'd be of that choice as I wandered aimlessly through throngs of tourists. Out of the corner of my eye I noticed a masked figure clad all in white carefully approaching me trying their best to look casual. I let a dagger the Leader had given me slide down my wrist and into my hand then turned into a nearby alley to limit civilian casualties. Shocking no one, the would-be assassin trailed me down the alley. It was then I noticed the red cross emblazoned on his mask.

"Really taking the Knight Templar bit seriously, huh? Who sends their regards this time?" I asked, inwardly preparing to fight.

"No regards, only vengeance!" the assassin said, two blades sliding down his wrists into his hands.

I laughed, then whistled a tune the Leader had me practice and three Dust materialized from the crowd.

Chapter 10 – Interrogation

I lunged at the assassin to keep him distracted long enough for my man in the purple suit to seize him. Wasting no time my fellow Dust yanked the man's mouth opened pulling out some kind of pill while a third Dust jabbed him with a thick needle, rendering him unconscious.

Together we escorted the sleeping assassin to a nearby hover-car and lowered him in the backseat.

People from the street started filming us with their phones so I covered my face with my hand while purple suit Dust explained the situation, "He's a drunk fellow street performer, nothing to see here." Some people bought the explanation and began clapping for our 'good deed' of helping him. *Handy that most people here are drunk tourists themselves.* I thought. We piled into the hover-car while our purple suit ally bound the would-be assassin's hands.

"That needle... what was in it?" I asked impressed.

"CIA tech obtained by the Keeper Above All." my ally explained.

"Interesting." I said while inspecting the assassin's blades; they were extremely simple in construction, probably cast from a mold and were very sharp. I opted to carefully pocket the knives to keep them out of civilian hands. After a while of carefully navigating foot traffic we arrived at a familiar parking garage. Once I got the secret passageway opened my allies dragged the assassin inside all the way to the Leader whom greeted us with a grandfatherly smile.

"What gifts do you bring me this day lads?" he asked.

"You were right sir, they were after me. Sent this fool to commit vengeance, or so he said." I explained casually.

"Alright, bind him to that chair. It's time we get down and dirty." The Leader grinned.

I stripped my would-be killer down to his underwear so he couldn't hide anything from us to help himself escape, then bound him tightly to an old wooden chair nearby. With the set-up done we waited until our new friend awoke.

When he started to stir, we all put on our masks, less for privacy, and more for the intimidation factor of it all. Taking the lead I drew his knives to taunt him then threw them aside before drawing the knife the Leader had given me. Mercilessly I pressed it to his throat until I drew blood.

"Tell us everything about your organization, and hurry... my hand might slip." I growled.

The assassin laughed as he chomped down on the pill that was no longer there. "Let it slip then." he said grinning.

The Leader pushed me aside, taking back his knife. "That's not how you interrogate someone..." he said, "*This* is how you interrogate someone!"

Hours later I couldn't blame our prey for crying, everything I'd just witnessed left me a little shaken as well. This Leader was a monster with a blade. Our prey sat there bound and bloodied in tears begging for the pain to stop.

"Speak. The truth will set you free!" the Leader said gently.

Surprisingly the assassin managed to chuckle. "There's a tracker in my tooth, my allies will be here any minute!"

The Leader laughed. "This area as well as the area surrounding it is electronically dampened. You can talk, or you can leave here in a body bag."

The assassin had begun to shake anew. "I am a Dagger of King Artorious, holy knight of the Knights Hospitaller. One of ours killed your Revy and planted your mask!"

I was enraged. "You what??"

"You think you stopped nuclear war, but you stopped nothing! We will cleanse the heathens from all lands and emerge the new rulers of this world!"

"Fool, what do you think will happen to your kind when the bombs drop? You have nowhere to hide, same as us. But if you're so willing to die you should be willing to elaborate on your forces."

The assassin coughed up blood when he laughed. "We are thousands. As we speak your Dust infiltrating China and Russia are being wiped clean. You cannot stop us! But don't fret over the bombs, you'll all die before then..."

"I've heard enough." The Leader said, slitting the assassin's throat. I was barely holding it together.

"Sir, what are we gonna do!? The war was supposed to be averted!" I exclaimed.

"Calm yourself, Dust. Your efforts weren't in vain. I'll task my forces to split up between the two countries to ensure mission success."

"Sir, bad news: our scouts report Chinese and Russian forces are slaughtering non-natives in droves. It will be highly difficult to send any reinforcements at all!" Purple suit Dust said.

"Damn." the Leader grimaced. "Send only those native to the respective country if possible. We can't abide nuclear war!"

They took a page out of Revy's playbook, huh? I thought, shaking my head in disbelief.

My allies busied themselves bagging up the assassin so I turned to the Leader. "Sir, what should I do?" I said, my voice shaking with fear.

The Leader looked grim, "Go home, Dust. Your presence here has served its ultimate purpose. If worse comes to worst I'd be content in knowing my peoples' affairs were in order."

"That's it? Just run home? We're a shadow cabal of professional assassins, can't we do something?" I pleaded.

"I *am* going to do something. I'll coordinate with worldwide leadership on bolstering Canada's war effort. In the meantime ask yourself not what Dust can do, but what Murphy Smith can do. You could report on the atrocities China and Russia are committing. Your words could force an international response!"

I doubt it, what soldiers will they respond with if any? The Dust are our only hope. But the Leaders will handle that... he's right... I have to try! I grabbed a USB stick from my suitcase and took copies of the evidence my ally had pulled up on the Leader's screens. *Now I just have to get home without getting killed. Then to work without getting killed. And finally get George to believe all of this, without getting us both killed. Oh joy.*

As though he was reading my mind the Leader spoke, "The Dust here will join you on your trip home and guard you until your work is published. Focus on the task at hand!" he said seriously.

"Yes sir, thank you sir." I said, turning to leave.

Flanked by my now temporary allies we carried the body bag out of the bunker, tossing it in purple suit's hover-car.

"Won't they track us now?" I asked worried.

"Yup, all the way to the dump." he replied casually. We off-loaded the body at a nearby dump then sped off to the airport where the Leader's private jet waited. I couldn't help wondering if our plane would be shot down by an Axis missile, but we were fine. *So far so good...* I thought. The sounds of ordinance and air raid sirens filled my ears. I found myself weirdly comforted by it all. *The sounds of home, I guess...* I mused. I stowed my mask in a secret compartment in my suitcase then we hailed a hovercab headed straight for CRBN news. When we arrived I tipped the cabby generously then hauled ass for George's office.

Hey boss, how's things?" I asked breathlessly.

"Ah yes, the star reporter returns. I was beginning to worry the war had gotten ya." George said belly-laughing.

"No, just busy..."

"The wife filled me in, no worries. Glad to have you back. Tell me you brought something big!"

I produced the USB drive. "Is war crimes to the extreme big enough for you?" I asked, passing him the drive.

"Holy balls, Smith... where'd you get all this?" George exclaimed.

"Drones." I said, unsure if I should elaborate. George understood the meaning in my silence though.

"I know a few sources we can quote. We have to publish this yesterday!"

Prime Minister Rudolfo Aziz sat in his basement office trying in vain to rally further support from allied nations when he got a text from Murphy Smith with a link. He opened the link and burst into a Cheshire grin. Rudolfo pulled up every official's number he could find and spammed the link to all of them, which admittedly wasn't necessary because the footage had already hit the international news. With the link he included a final plea: "Canada needs your support, if we fall democracy falls with us." For hours his phone remained ominously silent. Then a single reply came back from Canada's ambassador to the

UN: "Investigations against you have been halted for a time. The UN is voting on whether to provide direct aid now."

"Thank you." Rudolfo replied then busied himself watching Minecraft tutorials for a few hours till his phone went off like crazy. Representatives from the majority of allied nations with UN ties were pledging aid, mostly in the form of money as most officials had converted their armies into lifespan, but Rudolfo was heartened to see the less affluent nations still had troops to commit. *I suppose it pays that ImmortanWire licenses are so expensive.* Rudolfo thought. Wasting no time, he texted Murphy Smith to set up an exclusive press conference. It was time to welcome the new recruits.

Hours later CRBN camera crews were set and rolling. Rudolfo cleared his throat. "Canadians are grateful for the support of the UN and their allies. I have chartered military plans using the recent donations we've received to bring in foreign troops who will doubtless be the linchpin in saving our precious democracy. As you can hear, Axis forces still bomb us day in and day out, but we stand strong. I'm humbled every day by the stories of brave Canadians, like Julie, who shipped her infant son to Jamaica to visit family, while she and her three sisters took up arms to defend us all. Thank you, Julie, you're a true hero, as are all Canadians, who despite it all continue to go to work to keep our economy booming and our enemies seething. Whether you wear a business suit or fatigues you all have my utmost respect. In closing I've liquidated the rest of my Aziz Solar Systems holdings and am proud to announce that I'll match any donations to the Canada Strong fund up to thirty billion dollars. Thank you, and may the strength of our heroes save us all!"

After the camera crew left I stayed behind to check on the Leader. Wordlessly we went downstairs where Rudy waited happily.

"Thank you, Smith. Your work may've just saved Canada." the Leader said. *It's strange for him to address me by name.* I thought. "My pleasure sir. If I may ask: how will you fund operations now that you've officially dissolved Aziz Solar?"

"You forget I own MiraiCorp as well. Worry not, my future as well as the future of the Keepers and their Dust is secure."

"What can we do regarding the Knights Hospitaller assassins?" I asked, still weary of every shadowy alley I passed.

Smiling the Leader turned one of his monitors to face me, on which rioters in Russia and China were clashing with dwindling police forces and burning government buildings. The best part? They were all wearing our mask, or an approximation thereof.

"I don't think anyone, assassin or not, would dare try and enter government right now, let alone obtain sufficient power to fire nukes. The people have Canada's backs, whether they mean to or not." he explained.

"That's good news sir, but what's stopping the wannabe Knights Templar from cleansing the world of heathens some time after the war?" I tried to stifle my fearful frustration.

"You."

"Me, sir? You've lost me."

"You, Mr. Smith. For you exposed our enemy as real and allowed me cause to rally our worldwide Dust. You, whom poured fuel on the riots in Axis countries with your journalism, and said journalism that secured us all the funds we'll ever need to make our army the greatest in the world!"

I blushed, "Thank you, sir, that's high praise, but I really didn't do much."

"You've done a lot for a Dust my dear Revy brought in on a whim. You've done me proud."

"Thank you, sir. If I may ask, what's next?"

"You go home, live your life as a journalist. You've done more than enough, plus your face is too well known to be an assassin." The Leader said gently.

"Understood," I said, returning my mask, "but what about you?"

"It's time Canada rises up to cleanse the world." he said coldly.

I shuddered internally, "You don't mean?" I began.

"It's time to win this war to end all wars and bring our betterment to the world." he was shockingly resolute.

I decided then and there with great respect and naivety to believe in the man who'd spent countless years bettering lives, including my own, and thought about his words no further. I left for home as Murphy Smith, the life of a Dust put firmly behind me.

One Year Later

I was elated to be at town hall reporting as PM Rudolfo Aziz announced Canada's victory in the war to end all wars. He strode up to the podium to give a victory speech.

"Canadians and the world, I'm proud of all of you today. Your resolute determination from the salary-man to the protesters in China and Russia, to the new Presidents of those regions... You've all done the world a great service by fighting off tyranny and remaining true to yourselves even as bombs rained down upon us. Now the real work begins: we must rebuild. Our homes, our businesses, our economies, and our very lives were strained or lost due to cowardly delusional communists and their enablers. Never again! I denounce the assassinations of China and Russia's previous dictators, but not the mask of those who freed you all. Keep its visage in your hearts as a signal to any who would rise up against you. Know that everyone who fought for Canada is now a permanent Canadian, and anyone from anywhere can be one as well, one need only enlist. As of today, Canada becomes unstoppable. Dust, rage on to honour the dead. Thank you."

With that Rudolfo got in his limo headed for home leaving all questions unanswered. I felt like the world had collapsed around me. *I'll say in my piece that he misspoke, that he meant to say 'Just'. But did he just give the go ahead for his planted assassins to...* My eyes went wide, I'd begun to sweat. *There's no way to pin it on him, but when he said cleanse, he meant world leadership didn't he? The crazy man is taking over the world and no one will ever know!* But I knew, worse still I no longer had clearance to any of the bunkers, so if I wanted to fight, I couldn't. I also knew I couldn't publicly turn against him since his pardon was the only thing protecting me. I'd killed for the man, and in doing so I'd helped doom any semblance of real freedom anyone had. The Leader, Keeper Above All, now effectively ruled the world, it was only a matter of time. The next day news had begun to come in detailing various world leaders mysteriously ending up dead. The only thing linking the killings together was an all-too-familiar mask. I spent the day writing news reports, careful to remain impartial and professional. Provable facts only. I didn't sleep much anymore.

Chapter 11 – Holdfast

The Leader sat behind his desk in Quebec, his mask in a desk drawer for when the time came.

"Sir?" An RCMP unit and proud Dust asked when Rudolfo rang.

"Are they ready?" he asked seriously.

"Yes sir, all the Holdfasts are ready and stocked."

"Good." The Leader said, donning his mask, "Take me to the other Leaders. It's time."

"Sir, are you certain? People are rioting the world over, they blame Canada for the rash of recent assassinations – world governments blame you!"

"As they should. If they don't quiet down by the time our allies migrate to the Holdfasts my orders are thus: kill them all."

The RCMP Dust bowed, and the pair got in an unmarked car headed for the nuclear war bunker Rudolfo dubbed Holdfast 1.

Jonathan Aziz sat at home petting Rudy while he watched the news. When he heard his father's order to the Dust his jaw hit the floor. Wordlessly he let Rudy outside then hopped in his car bee-lining for Murphy Smith's place. He knocked on the door after a few hours of driving visibly winded from over-thinking.

The second I opened the door Jonathan pushed his way inside.

"Did you know he was doing this?!" Jonathan demanded.

I was visibly wrecked by stress. "No, he vaguely mentioned cleansing the world, but I figured he was speaking of terrorists et cetera, not our allied nation's leadership too!" I said flustered.

Jonathan looked just as caught unaware as I was. "He and mother vaguely opined an interest in authority, but she never would've allowed our allies to come under harm, regardless of how much scrutiny father was under..."

We two assassins sat flabbergasted like naive children for a time.

"I have to wonder was this always the Leader's plan? I mean truly?" I said, my fists clenched.

"Probably... Mother and Revy died for this?!" Jonathan growled.

"We have to stop him. Somehow we have to stop him." I exclaimed.

Jonathan's gray eyes went cold. "I will, he just invited me to check out his new bunker. I can get him alone there. What about you?"

I sighed. *I never would've thought the Holdfasts were for this, I thought they were a response to Axis nuke treats... to protect people!* "I'm going public with everything I know. If someone comes after me so be it, the world's gonna end soon anyway, and I wasn't invited to a Holdfast by our great Leader."

Silently Jonathan shook my hand then abruptly left as quickly as he came. I vaguely caught sight of a pistol under his jacket as he turned. Once he was long gone I set up a livestream on my precious gaming PC that I'd bought with the Leader's blood money.

I stifled tears as the stream went live.

"My Name is Murphy Smith, journalist and known assassin. Yes, all of you who doubted my pardon were right to do so. I killed the Russian dictator via poison. Why? Well in short under the command of my Leader, the Keeper Above All, also known as Rudolfo Aziz I did what I believed would save the world. I did so under the title of Dust. Yes, Dust. The name for each unit of our assassin group. This is significant because just recently the Leader knowingly commanded all Dust to rage forth – a public final order which I can verify did lead to the deaths of world leaders, both allied and not. All in the name of his ultimate goal: shadow world domination. That goal, I'm horrified to say, has been achieved. Goodbye, and good luck to all not invited to the Holdfasts."

I ended the stream in tears then turned on the news. As I'd hoped the stream was already in local news and would soon go global. *The perks of being someone under international scrutiny.* I thought. With my last job done I grabbed a pistol from under my mattress and waited. It wasn't long before someone banged on my door.

"Hell-" I started to say, trying to look out the view-port when bullets blasted through my door tearing me to bits.

Hours later Jonathan Aziz arrived at the Prime Minister's Holdfast. His father's RCMP escort helped him through the already massive throng of protesters, scanned him in, then went back to fighting off protesters. Shaken, Jonathan gathered himself. He pushed past other Dust that he vaguely recognized, past Leaders he'd grown up around, and finally after what felt like agonizing hours of glad-handing and pretending all was routine he was in his father's office. The office looked like all of Rudolfo's other offices except for a MiraiCorp ImmortanWire station in the corner.

"Father."

"D-Son. Welcome, you made it!" Rudolfo beamed.

"You hate me don't you?" Jonathan growled.

"What?"

"Oh come on dad, ever since I wanted to be your son you've hated me. Before the world ends you could at least be honest!"

"Fine, Joanna, I hate you, happy?!" Rudolfo boomed.

"Yes." With that Jonathan drew his pistol, shot Rudolfo in the head, then turned the gun on himself as his father's assassins closed in on him. The Aziz family was gone, but Rudolfo's chain of shadow command remained. Leader Valenti of Italy took his seat just as Canada's sirens went off anew.

"America has fired nukes!" he exclaimed laughing, "And so shall the other nuclear powers. Good riddance to all, and to all a good death." The Leader sat jovial surrounded by his loyal army assured in the fact no harm could come to them.

Chapter 12 – Many Years Later

The planet went to shit while the people with the resources to do something about it raced each other to the edge of space or hid underground. I live underground; I am a soldier. I have no name. The Generals just call out to me as "You there." That might change soon if I can survive the trials.

"You there!" a bearded General called.

"Sir?" all fifteen trainees replied in unison. I noticed him pointing to me, so I stepped forward.

"Your time has come. For eighteen years we've trained you; now you prove your strength in the trials!"

Smiling, I donned my gel bodysuit in front of everyone, along with the other trainees, and marched down the corrugated steel halls past our aging water purifier and greenhouse room to the forbidden zone – the blast door that sealed off the trial site. The door said "MiraiCorp".

General Zai – the bearded one – used his access card to unseal the trial site. What was inside shocked me: a sterile white room filled with reclined dentist-like chairs surrounded by robotic arms that held needles. General Zai gestured and I sat in the indicated chair, filled with nervous trepidation. Across the room another set of techno-chairs sat empty that I'd never seen before. General Zai gestured to get my attention.

"You were raised as one, now you become the other," General James began as the needles slowly descended towards us trainees in our sweat-drenched gel bodysuits. Pain seared through my whole body when the needles finally dug in. I could feel every muscle I knew burning while a persistent ache permeated in the background.

Eventually, I blacked out. I don't know how long the trials took, but by the smile on General Zai's face, it seemed I'd done okay.

"You there," he exclaimed, pointing at a delirious me. "You survived, and as such have passed the trials. As your sponsor, I name you Strength."

"Strength . . ." I muttered, smiling like a fool while I tried to stand. My body felt amazing, though when I looked down, I was shocked to find I was very different. The revelation caused me to pass out.

When I finally awoke, I found myself lying in a pitch-black room.

"I understand the transition is a trying one, but you're okay. When I turn the lights on, you'll be in your power armour and visible traits such as what shocked you so will be hidden," General Zai said.

Light blasted me in the face, but my helmet's visor kicked in and automatically acted like sunglasses, shielding my now enhanced sight. My eyes darted around the room as my panicked brain instinctively expected danger.

"You're fine, Strength, now rise," General Zai commanded gently.

I stood to attention, anchoring my eyes on General Zai, a person who'd been like a father to me. It calmed me slightly.

"Sir, if I may, where is everyone else?" I asked.

"Dead. Only you survived the trials," General Zai said, looking much younger somehow, a hint of sadness in his stoic delivery. Part of me wanted to cry for them, but ultimately, I just felt numb. All of us were just "You there". Not permitted any hobbies or distinguishing traits. Our lives were spent fighting each other, working out, and training at the shooting range. All to hone our bodies for this day when we'd pass the trials and emerge ready to reclaim the surface world for the Generals. Now I was the only survivor. I finally had a name: Strength. Doubtless, General Zai gave me this name to represent that he wanted me to be strong, which I'd have to be to reclaim any part of the supposedly desolate above-ground by myself.

Dread began to fill me. I knew the order was coming.

"Strength, your orders are to scout the surface for habitable land with water. Our purifier is failing. Now that it's just us Generals down here, we'll last a few months, but only if we're lucky. I've filled your suit's water reserves. To keep your suit's hydro-nuclear generator running, you'll need to keep up the water levels as much as possible. And remember: strenuous activity will drain the cell faster. Right now, you have three months of run time. Come with me." General Zai gestured and I followed, sure we'd be headed to the bunker's armoury.

Once General Zai buzzed us in, I was met with a familiar sight: guns, bows, knives, swords, ammo, more power armour suits, power cells, and practice dummies that were much worse for wear. Casually, I grabbed two combat knives, a sniper rifle, a collapsible compound bow, a short sword, and a quiver of twenty-four arrows. General Zai helped me strap the knives to the hips of my armour while General James strapped the sword, quiver, and rifle to my back. To finish the absurd ensemble, I filled my chest pouches with armour-piercing rifle ammo – ten mags of twelve rounds each.

I turned to look in the mirror. The armour left things like gender ambiguous, as it covered my whole body in tank-like white plating with red accents. My visor was a stretched V-shape and blood red. I looked like a garishly striking knight mixed with a super-soldier. I'd trained in de-powered armour before to feel how heavy two tonnes are without assistance, so I knew when the General cautioned about water, he meant it.

"This armour is your home, but if you don't heed it, this armour will be your tomb," General James would always caution.

"Sir, why do I need all of these weapons?" I asked, inwardly dreading the answer.

"Drone surveillance of a forty-kilometre radius shows multiple cities in Ontario have fallen to bandits. Close quarters combat is all well and good, but you have to be mindful of water usage, so it's better you be equipped to the hilt," General Zai reasoned.

"Did the drone give any indication of ground conditions?" I asked.

"Pollution is heavy, so keep your helmet on at all times unless safe or eating. The suit's electrolysis process will keep you supplied with oxygen. Heatwaves exceed the one-point-five-degree global projections, so grab water where you can to keep the suit running or the heat will dehydrate you in minutes. Finally, flash floods are common and the grounds are littered with West Nile carrier ticks during dry spells. You will want to steer clear of using filthy water if possible, to avoid gunking up your suit's systems, but if in a pinch, I put cloth filters in with your rifle ammo."

"Thank you, sir," I said as General James released my chest plate to show me the water intake valve one last time.

Once I selected the button on my hologram display of my visor with by blinking, the chest plate resealed. To top me off, General James handed me a bag filled with ration bars, some steel rope, and a Swiss army knife.

"Normally your suit would be forest camo-green, but as the last known representative of Canada, the greatest nation, we opted for our flag's colours."

"I'll stick out like a sore thumb . . ."

"Yes. But you're highly bullet resistant up to sustained fire from .50 calibre armour-piercing rounds, or even light RPG barrages. Neither of which are common among the rabble. Drone footage shows mostly small arms and makeshift weaponry can be expected," General James explained.

I sighed; the stoic reminder of my impervious state wasn't as comforting as he likely hoped.

"Strength, today you leave the bunker in the hopes that you'll find diplomatic solutions to our problems so that humanity can retake Canada for the next generation. The colours of your suit should ever remind you of that underlying purpose. Though if peace can't be had diplomatically, feel free to secure it as you see fit," General Zai finished as they led me one last time past the green room and water purifier towards the bank vault-like entrance to our home.

Both Generals keyed in their IDs and the vault-like door squealed open on its giant ribbed track. Blinding white light and a wave of heat met us. I nodded goodbye to General Zai, then charged headlong into the wastes while the door sealed behind me.

Powered up, my armour felt weightless despite weighing over two tonnes with my gear. I knew I only had three months, at best, to retake my Generals' country. Easy. At least, I hoped it would be. With my enhanced sight, I could make out a caravan being harassed by bandits. Two targets, distance 200m. I unfastened my rifle and loaded a magazine. Two shots, two kills. For a moment, I was proud of my proficiency until I saw the bloodied corpses with holes blown through their heads. I began to sweat, and I felt like vomiting. Growing up, we only trained at war; we only sparred together. Sure, the Generals showed us historical war footage, but that couldn't prepare me for taking a life. I took a minute to breathe.

One hundred eighteen rounds remained before I'd have to switch to my bow. Concentrating on my ammo count calmed me and kept me focused as I headed carefully toward the caravan, ready for its owner to turn on me. I expected a reaction of fear; after all, it's not every day a red-and-white fully armoured eight-foot-tall hulk of a person marches up to you.

"Hi," I said.

"Greetings," he replied, a rusty gun over his shoulder. He was about six feet tall and built like a bodybuilder, but had an easy smile under his handlebar moustache. He had two horses that towed a jerry-rigged trailer filled with assorted tools and parts.

"The name's Dave, many thanks for the save, what brings you to these parts?" he said.

"I'm Strength. Soldier of Canada under General Zai. My mission is to retake this land from the bandits and secure water for my people by any means necessary."

Dave looked at the corpses of the bandits then back to me like I was some sort of anomaly.

"I see that. Y' know, I can't make out who's under there due to the modulation of your voice. You a guy or girl?"

"I am Strength."

". . . Okay, Strength, well what say you to a temporary alliance. You keep us safe and I'll help you navigate Ravagok city. That's the bandit name for Toronto."

"Deal."

We walked for a good twenty minutes until we came upon a giant wooden gate. Dead bodies on pikes lined the roadside. Most of them were women who'd had their bodies exposed before death.

"Harlots," Dave explained sadly. "The Overboss Graveburn takes in women until they irritate him and this happens." I stayed silent but under my helmet, I felt enraged.

"In this world, you're either useful or you're meat," Dave finished as he knocked on the giant gate.

"Who is it?" a gravelly voice called out.

"Dave Johnson, with a guest."

"Oh! Dave, welcome back, bud. You fixing the boss's HVAC has him in a really good mood, you know!"

"Good to hear it, Jenkins."

Jenkins grunted as he pushed the giant gate open. When his eyes fell on me, his jaw dropped and he pulled out a dirty Glock.

"The hell are you?" he exclaimed.

"I am Strength," I said stoically.

"Put your gun down, Jenkins, they're here to see the boss," Dave said, smiling his easy smile.

"Like hell, they're clearly a warrior; if they're going anywhere, it's to the pits!"

"What are the pits?" I asked.

"A fighting arena created by the latest bout of flooding. Muddy ground, last man standing type deal. Winner gets an audience with the boss," Dave explained.

"Easy," I said.

"Then it's settled, follow me."

We followed Jenkins deep into the city, past hordes of dirty people who looked at me with a mix of awe and fear. Dilapidated skyscrapers lined the muddy streets. Old cars were strewn around the buildings, their fuel long since spent. Most buildings were in some state of water damage or disrepair, but the closer we got to what I assumed was the centre of the city, the more lively things began to look. Well-fed armed goons accosted makeup-wearing escorts advertising their bodies on the side streets and alleyways. Children played openly in the streets, unfazed by all the guns and adult activity around. I felt queasy as I'd only ever seen my fellow trainees nude, and the Generals always dressed properly, never carrying arms. The debauchery on display here was unbefitting of a Canadian city. Children deserved to be in training, kept away from the rabble until trial day . . . though I guessed trials didn't happen here outside of in the pits themselves.

Chapter 13 – The Pits

Maybe twenty minutes later we reached a sign that read: The Pits. This would be my second trial, and my one chance to negotiate for water. I hoped I wouldn't have to kill many people to get it, but the Generals were relying on me so I'd do what had to be done.

"Dave, buddy, can you come fix my fridge today?" a bulky man growled.

"Sure thing, Bruiser, right after I sign my friend here up for a round in the pits."

"Name?"

"Strength."

"Seriously?"

"Your name is Bruiser..."

"Fair. Fine, you're signed up. No rules, go in, kill, get out alive. Simple. See you in the pits tomorrow."

The Next Day

My body ached furiously. Living in the armour wasn't ideal even with my gel bodysuit. Though admittedly, being armoured left me feeling confident – impervious even. I guessed I'd find out how true that was soon enough.

"Good morning!" Dave said, having met me in his living room. Dave lived in the penthouse of one of the few skyscrapers in good repair, a perk of being the guy the boss calls to fix stuff.

"Why'd you let me stay here?" I asked.

"I figured you had nowhere to go. And if you wanted to hurt me, you wouldn't have saved me from those bandits yesterday. Don't overthink it." He smiled his easy smile. I relaxed, then set about checking my gear. Once that was done, we headed back to the entrance of the pits, where Bruiser was waiting with an eerie smile.

"Last chance to back out," he said.

"I'm fighting," I replied.

"So be it."

With that, the doors were pulled open by Bruiser's goons. Inside was an utter shit show of chaos: downed buildings, dead bodies, and people milling about with their guns drawn on each other. I'd heard gunshots all night long from Dave's place, so a bunch of corpses being here didn't much shock me. But I was surprised by the number of men, women, and even children still standing. Disturbingly, all the kids were armed. For their sake, I drew my rifle to try to look intimidating before I spoke. "Retreat now all of you and I'll let you live!" I yelled.

Jeers and laughter permeated the muddy street. Over the laughter, a bull-horn sounded. "Kill the fancy one and bring me that armour. Anyone who fails to try will be executed," a deep voice boomed.

I figured that had to be Graveburn. I could see a light coming from a pristine skyscraper in the distance, outfitted with a PA system. If I survived, that's where I'd be headed next. To my dismay, no one retreated, in fact, Bruiser let more people in, himself included.

"Fine," I muttered and opened fire. I had 117 rounds . . . 105 . . . 93 . . . 81 . . . I stood my ground as my rifle sang out 69. Then my rifle jammed, so I drew my sword. I was rushed on all sides by men, women, and kids with an assortment of weapons. Every shot they fired pinged off of my armour like it was nothing. The whole time I stood there, I found myself worried the kids would be caught in the crossfire or hit by a deflected shot meant for me. I cut down three men. Inadvertently, I stood in the epicentre of a circle of corpses. Some bandits backed off momentarily, so I skillfully cleared the jam in my rifle with one fluid motion, sheathed my sword, and resumed firing into the unnervingly growing crowd of adults. 57 . . . 45 . . . 33 . . . 21. Another jam. I found myself wondering how many people there were in this shithole of a city. I cleared the jam with less than two mags left. Calmly, I resumed counting till the click of my rifle sang zero. Yet more still came.

I drew my sword in one hand as I dropped my rifle and vaulted over the shallowest pile of corpses. Screaming children that I'd ignored up to that point and let attack me, insisted on following. So in between stabbing and cutting through terrified adults, I systematically disarmed any child I could reach and spent any ammo they had into whom I could only assume were their parents. Counting each kill kept me focused and distracted me from the growing anxiety I felt. I found myself wondering if the water was even worth it; these people couldn't even hurt me. It was a tragic mismatch. The enemy numbers began to thin as I slashed away at what remained. My pristine red-and-white armour was splattered with blood and mud from all the combat manoeuvres and death I'd dealt.

After countless desperate people lay slain at my hand, I decided enough was enough. I'd push to the tower and kill the Overboss myself. The wails of crying children chased me as I charged toward the tower. I had to make this all count. Upon entering the Overboss's tower, I was met with heavy resistance. So, floor by floor, I warned, negotiated, and killed my way upward. My conscience was growing heavy; all I could think about were the crying, scared kids I left in the dust. But any attempt to dissuade my foes from meeting their untimely end fell on terrified, deaf ears. Eventually, I went back to silently counting until finally, after twenty floors, I found the penthouse and effortlessly kicked in the door.

Overboss Graveburn sat on a throne made of wood and a car's seat. I was bothered by the fact that he sat alone, smiling.

"You're good. Join me?"

"You should've asked that before sicking your scared people on me." I walked towards him, enraged.

"What are ya doin'?!" he said, shaking.

"Finishing this fight." I rammed my sword through his neck, then casually decapitated him. As I walked back down through the building, carrying Graveburn's head, the wails of children in my mind quieted ever so slightly. A notification on my visor warned me that I had one month of charge left. I'd burned two months of fuel just in one fight. I could feel myself beginning to sweat nervously; what if I couldn't find water? Shoving the thought from my mind, I reemerged into the pits and carefully stepped around all of the fresh corpses. I felt horrible. Thoughts of regret and doubt swirled in my mind. Had any of it mattered?

I counted twenty children all eyeing me with a mixture of fear, awe, and hatred. Then I saw Dave casually jogging into the pits.

"Are you here to fight?" I warned.

"God no, I'm here to congratulate our new Overboss, Strength."

I grimaced. "I don't want to be Overboss, I'm a soldier."

"You've no choice, bud. You toppled the king and so become king. Simple."

In full view of all survivors, I hoisted Graveburn's head and tossed it into the pits. "You're all free from fear. No longer will anyone command you to fight or die. Live on!" I ordered. I don't know if I expected cheers or adulation, but mostly people just stared.

Suddenly someone yelled, "All hail Overboss 200!" and people erupted into cheers. Men and women rushed me, exposing themselves to try to gain favour.

"Enough!" I commanded. "I've no interest in sexuality or being Overboss . . . and why 200?"

"To commemorate the over 200 you slew today!" the man said. It made me wonder what Graveburn did to earn his name.

"Dave, you're my second-in-command as of now. Where can I get water?" I asked.

"Follow me," Dave said, and together we exited the pits. I wasn't eager to come back. A horde of abandoned and orphaned children chased us.

"Go home," I commanded.

"We have no homes thanks to you . . ." one boy said and glared. I looked at Dave, who shrugged.

"I have an idea; come with me. We'll get water later," I said.

I led my group to Dave's cart. Without instruction, he cleared the cart and loaded the kids on.

With that done, we began the roughly twenty-minute trek to my old home. When we got there, the vault-like door was sealed. I waved at the security camera. Moments later, the door creaked open, revealing a smiling General Zai.

"Sir, I've taken an enemy base with access to water. I request that you take these children in and prepare them for the trials," I reported calmly, with my hands behind my back.

"Good work, Strength. I'll gladly take in new recruits, though our water purifier won't like the strain . . . I suppose that won't matter much longer." He turned from me to the children in Dave's cart.

"Today you are no one. You will be called *You There* until such time as you pass the trials. I am General Zai, your new father. You will obey me wholeheartedly or you will die. Any questions?" No one spoke, either out of fear or spite. I could tell by the look in one boy's eyes he'd be hard to train. Once the children were led into my home, General Zai turned to me.

"Strength, your orders are to hold your new position and build up a fighting force to expand outward. Also, I want regular shipments of water brought here weekly." I looked to Dave and he nodded.

"Any questions?" General Zai asked.

I nodded. "I need weapons."

Together with General Zai, I loaded Dave's cart with guns and blades. With that done, I saluted the General, turned on my heel, and we left.

"What are the trials?" Dave asked.

"A process by which a child becomes a soldier," I said casually.

"Is it safe?"

"No, of the last batch I was the only survivor . . ."

"Are you sure that's a good idea for those kids then?!"

"It's all I know . . . In this they have a chance, otherwise, they would've died as orphans. It's the best I could do for them."

Dave didn't seem convinced, but he just shrugged and broke out into a random song about his horses. I wasn't listening.

When we got back to Ravagok, I had to wade through crowds of people calling me 200 and throwing themselves at me. Dave helped me get water for my suit, then we focused on getting the weapons into my new skyscraper.

"What's next, boss?" Dave asked.

"Now we pyre the dead."

Dave chuckled. "Are you sure you don't want to strip them and put them on spikes?"

I just glared at him under my helmet. The silence said enough.

"Good idea, I'll gather dry wood."

We set about building a massive pyre, then loaded all of the bodies on it. Dave looked at me, I nodded, and he tossed the match. A while later, the air was filled with acrid smoke. I couldn't smell anything, but I looked at Dave, and he was crying.

"Are you okay?" I asked.

"Some of them were my friends . . ." Dave said.

"I'm sorry."

"You may've killed them, but it wasn't your fault. That bastard Graveburn caused this. And now he's dead, so vengeance is pointless!"

"Save your energy. You'll need it for training."

"You gave the people your word they'd be safe; no more forced war!"

"I did. And I meant it. Only volunteers will be trained and guaranteed water. I have orders to expand our reach."

"Expand it to where exactly?"

"I'm to retake Canada for the Generals."

"They expect one person to reunite a country? Suicide mission much?"

"Not as long as I can keep my armour stocked with water."

"So what if you're basically bulletproof, one person can't handle all that death!"

"I can." I said it assuredly, but I wondered if he had a point.

Chapter 14 – All That Death and More

"What are your hobbies, boss?" Dave suddenly asked me.

"What?" I replied.

"What are your hobbies? You must like to do something."

"War."

"And?"

"War."

"You're messing with me."

"Negative. I was raised for war; I live for war."

"Again, I have to ask: you think that's a good life for those kids?! Seriously?"

"Yes. It's their best chance at life in this world. They were already being raised for combat; this will simply strengthen them and prepare them for success."

"You're mad," Dave grumbled.

I was irritated. "And? What are your hobbies?"

"I sing."

"I noticed, and how does that prepare you for survival in this world?!"

"It doesn't . . ."

"So it's useless to worry about hobbies. As you said: one is useful or they're meat."

Dave looked sad. "You're wrong. A person needs a thing that brings them joy, especially in this world."

Although Dave stood six feet tall and was built like a bodybuilder, at that moment, he appeared to have the innocence of a child. He noticed I was ignoring him as we headed to the pits, so he broke into a song about puppy dogs and peace or some such. I wasn't listening. All I could think about was the hate in that boy's eyes. Would he find Dave's joy as a soldier? It wasn't my place to question. General Zai would make great warriors of each of those kids; warriors we'd need for the fights to come. I'd done the right thing. Dave was wrong.

Once we reached the pits, Dave handed me a bullhorn. "People of Ravagok, I am Strength. I'm seeking an army to advance through Toronto and retake it as a great hub of Canada! Any volunteers will train under me and be guaranteed water. However, I promised you all peace, so no one will be conscripted. I say again: service is completely voluntary, guaranteed weapons and water during training and service. Should no one volunteer, I'll do it myself." I lowered my bullhorn and waited. People milled around me, going about their days with fear in their eyes when they looked my way. After twenty minutes, no one had volunteered. Only fools hoping to garner favour dared approach. I dismissed them all. Meat was of no use; I needed the useful.

"The mass murderer Overboss 200 preaches peace?! Do you think we're stupid, or fool enough to be patriotic to a dead country? The Canadian government abandoned us all to hide underground with the rich elite. Did you forget that??!" a big blonde man shouted. I was shocked at his bravery to face me and by what he said.

"I was taught little of the surface world . . . But you're wrong, the government has not abandoned you. As we speak, the Generals train more to be like me, to be strong, to be ready to civilize the surface!" I said strongly.

"Ah yes, the twenty children you abducted after murdering their families! No doubt they're being brainwashed into being as dumb as you! Fuck your army, do it yourself!" The man flipped me off then marched away; a cohort of nervously like-minded followed in his stead.

Dave chuckled anxiously. "Well, looks like you made yourself an army alright, one that stands against you. Look, he's even taking your guns."

"Worry not. I have all of the armour-piercing rounds," I said, gesturing to my retrieved and somewhat muddy rifle. "Democracy is, as ever, built on disagreement. Tell me, will you let me train you, or would you rather stay everyone's best friend, Mr. Fix-All?" I asked seriously.

Dave huffed. "Fine, train me. Can't hurt to have more skills."

One Month Later

Dave sang, shot, and sliced his way through my rigorous training regiment, becoming highly proficient with his new rifle. I almost broke his wrist during CQC training. My armour and augments made me super strong, so I had to be very careful not to cause undue harm. Unfortunately, he was weak in CQC so I decided he'd be my sniper and spotter. That way he'd stay out of direct danger for the most part. Thanks to Dave's many contacts around the city from his days as a handyman, we'd conjured up ten trainees: four men and six women, and just enough guns to arm them. For the most part, I kept them doing generic target practice since most of them, especially the women for whatever reason, were experienced brawlers. Dave offhandedly mentioned that they had to be tough these days to avoid being assaulted.

Our unit would come under fire far sooner than Dave or I had hoped, thanks to the untimely approach of the blonde man who'd accosted me a month prior. He approached with a band of fifteen, all armed with my guns.

"200, we've come for your head! Your reign is over, child abductor!"

I held up my hand to stay my people. "If you want to fight for my position, we do it right here, one on one. Know this either way: the children are well cared for living in a bunker just twenty minutes from here should any of their family remain."

The man began shooting at me, so I charged him empty-handed to draw errant fire away from my people. I grabbed his rifle, wrenched it out of his hands, and deftly slammed its butt into the bridge of his nose, knocking him out in one blow.

Still glaring at me, his cohorts dropped my guns in surrender, which Dave's crew smoothly gathered.

"Boss, are you sure it's wise to let him live, knowing of your home?" Dave asked.

"It may seem unwise on the surface, but if the Generals sense a threat, they have armour like mine. They, as well as the children, will be safe. This way, when he wakes, we can attempt a more diplomatic approach. I'd like to avoid adding to my body count today if possible. I'm tired of hearing pained cries in my sleep," I said sadly. Dave gave me a curious look but didn't push me; the look in his eye betrayed a hint of understanding. When the blonde man finally awoke, I faced him.

"Name?" I asked.

"Steven," he said.

"Alright, Steven, our conflict ends here. Feel free to go see the children if you're worried." With that, I walked away, and Dave followed.

"What now, boss?" Dave asked.

I brandished my sword. "The city is yours; now I go to take back this province," I said as I marched away.

Eighteen Years Later

I'd shot, stabbed, chatted, and bashed my way through city after city, taking on the strongest of opponents to secure my position as their Overboss, only to leave and do it all again. I'd done well to keep my suit watered so no one could really touch me. It was too repetitive to bother giving much consideration; much like my recurring nightmares . . . so many corpses I'd lost count. One after another, their screams filled my dreams, their vengeful souls haunting me and threatening to pull me apart at the seams. I'd long since run out of ammunition. Most of my arrows were so blunted as to be useless, and my sword threatened to break with each brutal swing. Finally, I'd made it to the Parliament building in Quebec. The streets were dark and full of corpses.

People milled around me excitedly like I was some sort of star attraction, ignoring the detritus around us. Many coughed and retched like the plague had struck them, for it had: the zeta covid variant was still going strong. One of the many reasons General Zai cautioned me from removing my armour at all costs. The Canadian government had failed to procure vaccines in time, so the variants had mutated rapidly in the vaccine-hesitant. If any government still remained here, I hoped they were still working on covid, and West Nile ticks, and the streets of chaos. But here I stood alone instead of part of an army the way I was raised to be. Soldier of misfortune, I walked alone. The Parliament building stood – an ominously silent monolith from a bygone time. Nary a light shone in a single one of its windows. A tattered Canadian flag flapped proudly in the wind, casting a shadow on my scratched armour coloured in its image.

Seeing abandoned military vehicles and the sheer state of the nation's capital left me doubting myself. I couldn't tell if all the blood I'd shed in the name of my Generals' flag had accomplished anything. Can there really be a country if one must kill hordes of its people to retake it? I supposed it was too late to stop now. I'd left all of my easy allies behind, one after the other, in charge of the battlefields I'd turned Canada's cities and towns into. Although, as I approached Parliament, flanked by people begging for my attention to fight for them, get them water, cheering me on facetiously or whatever, I couldn't help feeling like this war wasn't my fault. War never changes and soldiers never stop fighting, whether on a battlefield or in a world of their mind's tortured making. Everyone wants a leader sometimes. Here I was, hoping some leadership still held a vestige of control, if only to make this fight worthwhile.

I searched Parliament for hours with my new cohort of stragglers, coming up dry. I collapsed to my knees, crying. None of it had mattered, after all. The government had truly abandoned us all underground. Where did General Zai get his orders, or had he made it all up to give us structure? Dejected, I helped my new friends get water, even fought some fights to blow off steam, then I realised what I should do next: It was time to go home.

Chapter 15 – Warriors Stored in a Vault

Days later I'd made it back to Toronto/Ravagok. After pestering a few timid locals, I learned Dave was working on someone's stove downtown. Mr. Fix-It struck again. Despite it all when I finally saw him, I smiled. Of course, he couldn't see that through my helmet, so I simply waved.

"Howdy, boss, how goes it?" he said, smiling his easy charming smile.

"The capital has long since fallen. Every city is the same mix of desperation, detritus, death, and misery. I'm an abandoned war machine for a silent legislative factory," I said sadly.

Dave grew serious. "And what did it cost you?"

"Everything."

"Not true, you're still alive."

"For what?!"

"To fight on. So what if the old government is gone, we're still here. You've liberated so many people, built mini governments like I humbly run here. It counts, all of it, I'm sure of it."

"I hope you're right. Hundreds disagree when I close my eyes to sleep."

"Forgive the rage we imagine for the dead, it's the only way forward," Dave suggested.

"How wise, Mr. Overboss," I said jokingly.

"Why, thank you, fellow Overboss."

"So what now?"

"Now I go home. I need answers only General Zai can provide. From there, who knows."

"Mind if I tag along?"

"Aren't you busy enough here?"

"Sure, but I get the sense you need me there even if you can't say it," Dave said, smiling as he wiped the sweat from his brow.

"Thanks, grab your rifle, let's get going!" I ordered.

Together, we marched in silence back to my home, a place I hadn't seen in years. I wondered how the children I left with General Zai and General James fared. It had been eighteen long, bloody years; doubtless, their trials were coming up. I found myself feeling tired and apprehensive. Would any of them survive? Would they remember me, and if so, would they favour or revile me?

Twenty minutes later, Dave and I stood at the vault-like door to my home. As it slowly creaked open, I felt anxious, like a guilty child. I'd failed in my mission technically since much of rural Canada remained under bandit control. General Zai greeted me in full black armour with two armoured individuals I didn't recognise, but I did recognise their camo-green armour. These were new soldiers.

"Strength, may I introduce Compassion and Integrity, the only survivors of the twenty children you brought us so long ago." I saluted the General and was saluted in turn by the new soldiers, which felt awkward.

"Sir, I have a report," I said.

"Go ahead, Strength," General Zai responded.

"I cleared out enemy leaders from all of the major cities, leaving only rural holdouts. In their place, I installed locals favourable to our cause, such as Dave here. Regrettably, the capital is gone. Left for last, I fear I was too late. If there were any government personnel still there, they're long gone."

"Understood. Don't worry too much about the rural forces. I'll task Integrity to clear that up once we move to the capital."

"Sir, if I may, where is General James?"

"Dead. He died during a training accident ten years ago."

"I'm sorry to hear that; he was a good man and better teacher."

"Indeed; we tried to get word to you but Dave mentioned during one of his weekly water deliveries that you'd left Toronto long ago. Ultimately, I decided against pursuing the matter so as to avoid distracting you from your mission."

I felt devastated; not only was General James gone but eighteen of the twenty kids I'd hoped to save were gone too. Was two people saved enough to make up for hundreds dead? I could only hope so.

"Other than yourself, sir, where do our orders come from?" I asked knowing full well the buildings of government were home to squatters now.

General Zai considered my query for a moment then said, "Follow me."

General Zai led, flanked by Compassion and Integrity, with Dave and I bringing up the rear. We passed the long since broken water purifier, the thriving green room, living quarters, and the now barren armoury to the most off-limits part of my home: the General's quarters. Once inside, we were faced with an array of monitors showing drone feeds, a spartan living quarters, and a dark area sealed with a bulkhead door simply labeled "MiraiCorp".

On approach, a laser shot from the bulkhead door, scanning General Zai's eyes, then it groaned open. I was shocked by what was inside: a giant catacomb filled with pipes and machinery, all coalescing around what looked like a glass war table. Projecting from the table was a gently pulsing blue laser orb. When we approached, the orb took on a vaguely humanoid face and spoke.

"Welcome back, General Zai."

"Thank you, ma'am," General Zai said.

"Soldiers at attention! This AI represents your Prime Minister Jill Corkus," General Zai commanded.

We all saluted, including, humorously enough, an awkward Dave who used the wrong hand. I could tell from the readings on my visor that the room was extremely hot, likely due to all the hardware around us. Dave wouldn't last long without armour.

"At ease," the AI PM Corkus said.

"Prime Minister, your soldier Strength has done a valiant job retaking key positions throughout the country these past eighteen years. They requested to know where our orders come from, so I brought them to you," General Zai explained.

"A wise decision, General. Greetings, Strength. I am where you get your orders from. General Zai and my drones have done well to keep me appraised of your exploits these past years. As such, I'll allow any questions you may have," PM Corkus said.

I bristled with excitement in my armour; the government did exist and its head had deigned to speak with me!

"Honourable Prime Minister, is the rest of the government intact somewhere?" I asked eagerly.

"Just call me Jill, Strength. Unfortunately, we're all that's left. Zeta covid, West Nile, and civil wars around lockdown restrictions wiped out most officials while the rest are M.I.A."

I was greatly dismayed. My hopes of reinstating the government seemed dashed. Nevertheless, I pressed forward as I was trained to. "That being the case, what are my orders, ma'am?"

"Your orders are to continue doing as you have done. Re-conquer our territory and reinstate our allies in positions of leadership. Now you'll have General Zai, Compassion, and Integrity to personally aid you in this herculean effort. General Zai, you're to take up a leadership position in Parliament so that people have an authority figure to look up to. That's all I have to say, you're all dismissed."

We all saluted and left the bunker for the outside world. Dave was relieved to be outside in the open air once more.

Night had fallen, so we opted to make camp outside my home.

"Are you sure you don't want some armour, Dave?" General Zai asked.

"I doubt I'd survive the process to earn it based on what Strength mutters about in their sleep," Dave admitted. I was embarrassed; I didn't know I was a sleep talker.

"You should've got a new suit, Strength. That one's got more pits in its armour plating than a field of plums. We still have ten left over," General Zai lectured.

"I'm fine, sir. This suit has served me well. Besides, you'll need the suits for future recruits," I said.

General Zai laughed heartily. "You're right, you're right." I noticed Dave eyeing Integrity closely; when I looked their way, their stoic demeanour seemed to bristle. I chalked it up to first mission jitters and gave Dave a gentle nudge.

"I'll be back, gonna scout for bandits . . ." Dave said, grabbing his rifle as he went. I couldn't help feeling something was off with him. He didn't seem to like Integrity or Compassion much.

General Zai yawned. "Time to turn in. Integrity, you're on first watch, Compassion, second."

"Sir!" they said in unison. Exhausted, I quickly fell asleep, feeling more safe than I ever had.

Some time later, I woke to an impact alert from my visor. Standing there was Integrity with their rifle pointed right at my face. My muscles tensed, but Integrity held up a finger in warning to stay me.

"Integrity, stand do—" General Zai began, only for the crack of an armour-piercing .50 calibre bullet leaving Compassion's rifle and hitting his visor to silence him prematurely. Coldly, Compassion approached.

"Why?!" I asked incredulously.

Integrity removed their helmet, revealing a blue-eyed blonde lady staring at me with a rage that felt familiar. Then it hit me. Those were the eyes of one of the boys I brought to General Zai.

"THIS IS WHY!" he screamed, indicating his body. "First you murdered my entire family, then you left me alone with that dictator Zai whose chemicals turned me into this!"

"Integrity, he's gone; stand down and we can talk . . ." I began.

"My name is Barnabus, I. Am. A. Man . . . I only played along with that monster Zai's training because I thought I'd be trapped underground with him forever; he never warned us what the trials would do . . . Then you showed up yesterday . . . that was when we realised we could act!" Barnabus kept his rifle levelled at my head as he ranted. I lay there assessing my situation, wondering whose reflexes were faster.

"Steven came a few years back, but he couldn't convince Zai to let us free in his care. Before he left, all he said was: 'Remember who you are'. And I did; I remembered you in your damned armour too. All white and red with my parents' blood, along with countless others. I vowed if I ever saw you again, I'd kill you!"

Suddenly a shot rang out and Compassion dropped like a log, but not before their rifle went off in their death grip as they fell. In that instant, I slapped Barnabus's rifle away and used my legs to knock him down as I rolled to my feet. He fired, but his shot hit the dirt beside my head. We engaged in desperate CQC, exchanging brutal blows while I kept his rifle in mind. Eventually, I got the upper hand and punched Barnabus square in the nose with more than enough force to knock him out.

Once the melee died down, I took a second to breathe. Maybe Dave was right, I should've killed Steven back in Toronto; maybe then things would've turned out differently. Dave! Was he okay? Ignoring the unconscious Barnabus, I rushed to where the first shot came from and found Dave lying on the ground, bleeding profusely from a chest wound. Compassion's dying shot had hit its vengeful target.

"Help . . ." Dave said weakly when he saw me.

Wordlessly, I picked him up and slung him over my shoulder, then rushed to General Zai's body. With both bodies in hand, I used General Zai's credentials to open my home, then rushed them to the Prime Minister's bulkhead. I removed General Zai's helmet and let the door scan the one eye he had left, then I gently let his body drop for now. I'd pyre him later; right now, I had to hope our AI Prime Minister knew some sciency way to help Dave.

"Ma'am, Dave's dying, please help," I begged.

"Greetings, Strength, unfortunately I can't help his body but I can save his mind." I looked at Dave by my side and he nodded.

"Lay him on my war table now." I did as the PM bid as fast as possible. Her blue laser face dissolved into a laser grid, which methodically scanned Dave's head. I held his hand through the process, feeling his grip weaken with each passing second.

"Hang on, Dave! That's an order . . ." I exclaimed.

"No worries, boss, the PM's got this," Dave said, smiling his easy smile one last time. Then I heard his last breath leave his lips and saw his eyes go glassy.

Even after all the death I'd dealt, the events of this night left me feeling numb.

"Done," the PM said.

"Done what?!" I almost yelled as tears threatened to flood my helmet.

"I've constructed an AI based on scans of Dave's brain and added my repository of knowledge. If you accept, I can put his data chip in your helmet so the two of you can still go on missions together?" she asked.

"Do it. Please," I said, remembering my place.

"Doing this will drain my power reserves. From here on out, it'll just be you and Dave, who will be powered by your suit . . ." she explained.

"Understood. Please continue."

A mechanical arm descended from the ceiling of the PM's catacombs. It drilled open a slot in my helmet that had previously been sealed and a glowing green circuit chip was slid in place before the cover was screwed back on. With that done, the PM's blue laser head faded away, leaving me presumably alone in the dark.

"Dave?" I asked quietly.

"AI David Johnson reporting for duty, boss!" I saw Dave's grinning face in two dimensions projected on the inside of my visor alongside system readings. I practically jumped for joy – he was back, in a way.

"I'm so glad, Dave . . . I'm sorry, it seems all my murdering led to your death . . ." I said sadly, looking at Dave's discarded body.

"No worries, Strength. Everything happens for a reason, and I feel hella smart now," he said reassuringly. "Now, let's go take care of business."

I marched from the dead PM's catacombs and gathered General Zai's body and a chain from the armoury. When we got outside, Barnabus was still out for the count. So, I hogtied him with the chain and used a combat knife to sever his water reserve by stabbing between his neck and his chest plate. With my slow vengeance assured, I stripped General Zai of his armour and set about building a pyre.

Once the flames began to dance, I let my tears flow once more. My father figure was gone, the Canadian government dead, and its last representative gave her 'life' to help my only friend, whom I also inadvertently got killed. Now it was just us.

"Why'd you pick me over the General?" Dave suddenly asked.

"General Zai's brain was half-destroyed by the shot that killed him. The Prime Minister explained she could only help a brain, and you only had a chest wound – the choice made itself," I explained.

"I'm grateful y'know."

"Okay . . ."

"What do we do now, Dave?" I asked, exasperated.

"I say we go back to Parliament and instate the new PM."

"Who?"

"You, Strength!"

I was incredulous. "I can't be Prime Minister, I'm just a soldier!"

"Same difference these days. Look, you liberated most of the country personally already and have allies from here to the US border, with you to thank for their positions. And the PM died believing in you. It has to be you," Dave reasoned.

"I'll consider it," I said, finally.

My helmet was beginning to fog from my tears. Ignoring General Zai's warning when I first left home, I removed it and turned the visor towards me so Dave could 'see' me.

"Wow, you're pretty, Miss Strength!" he said. I looked at my reflection in my dirty, scratched, glossy red visor. I had big blue eyes and flowing red hair.

"Just Strength," I said sternly as I aired out my helmet, then quickly put it back on. We stayed the night at General Zai's pyre. I stocked up on water from one of Dave's earlier supply runs, then we left for Parliament to begin the real fight: creating a peaceful future government out of this shit show of a world.

Chapter 16 – Family; Planet: Helix-6

I was playing *Dead City 7,* just driving my blood-red sports car around while my buddies mowed down pedestrians. Good times.

"Cow!" my buddy Daveed called out over the mic as he ran over an obese black woman with a hijacked city bus. "1000 pointz, dude!" he exclaimed cheerfully.

"Cole Sanburg, get down here!" my mom demanded.

I sighed, said bye to the homies, and logged out. I blinked hard, trying to shake the pain in the back of my brain. Rubbing my reddened eyes, I turned off my monitor, then glanced around my room. It was a sty. A dusty black curtain hung over my window to keep out the pesky sunlight. In the darkness created by the absence of my monitor's light, I could vaguely make out piles of dirty clothes as well as posters of my favourite nude models on my walls.

Straining myself, I just barely managed to transfer from my gaming chair to my electric wheelchair.

I huffed. Transfers were getting harder by the day. I glanced at my weights by my bed and gave them a dirty look. *Nothing's helping,* I thought. *Doctors said Cerebral Palsy didn't get worse, but they gotta be full of it.* Musing about my disability wasn't helpful, so I turned my wheelchair on. *Please work...* A familiar beep from the chair was followed by a glorious sign of success: a robotic arm extended from under my left armrest, then a light array on the end of the arm lit up revealing a holographic figure of a woman. She was a well-endowed redhead I modelled after one of the posters on my wall resulting from a program I wrote called Live Your Lust Always, or Lyla for short. My smile beamed brighter than the lights that projected her black-leather-bodysuit-clad image for me.

"Greetings, Cole ..." she said in a sultry voice.

"Status please," I said.

"Batteries are at 90% with an effective runtime of three days at this rate of power drain. Wheelchair functions read as good, you're free to go."

"Dismissed," I said, and the robotic arm withdrew, leaving me alone in an ostensibly normal electric wheelchair.

I rode the house's elevator down to the main floor and found my mom standing there with her arms crossed. Below her scowl, she wore her normal smart business attire. I knew a lecture was coming.

"Well, what have you been working on?" she started.

"Lyla, and gaming ..." I admitted nervously.

"Show me."

"LYLA awaken, code Cole." Moments later, Lyla stood on her robotic arm, smiling at my mom.

Mom scoffed. "I give you access to multi-billion dollar AI tech and you use it to make an... e-slut?! Are you kidding me? And let me guess, when you aren't fawning over her, you're wasting time playing video games, right?"

"Right ..."

"Cole, Dyptherion Inc. needs minds like yours focused on something other than hormones and distractions. We're at war for crying out loud! Or did you forget?"

"No ..."

Mom huffed. "Enough of this; I have to go to work. See you tomorrow." With that, she stomped away in her high heels.

I heard her tubby-looking space shuttle take off. Mom was the CEO of Dyptherion Inc., a previously well-known medical supplies company turned weapons manufacturer after NASA discovered our new home planet Helix-6. Earth had been mostly abandoned after much of the planet was rendered in-habitable by global warming and nuclear war; that was until a new element was discovered growing in the swamp lands that hadn't yet been paved over. It turned out that in the planet's desperation to purify the air from humanity's pollution, swamps around the world had turned that pollution into a red gel-like substance called Dyptherite. Mom had been the one to discover the ele-ment and it was her work that unlocked its mutagenic and unstable properties, first for medical purposes, and then of course, for weaponry – humanity never learned... my family was no less guilty of this.

Thanks to Mom's work in conjunction with NASA, humanity escaped to Helix-6 before Earth fully gave up the ghost. Now we lived in a post-modernist white brick mansion off the coast of Eden city, the capital of Helix-6. The planet was brimming with beautiful lush jungles and crystal-clear oceans, as if the Amazon rainforest had been cloned in its prime and pasted all over a blank canvas. On weekends Mom and I used to take shuttle trips around the planet to take it all in under its ginormous sun, but we stopped doing that in recent years, partly out of boredom and an admittedly ironic distaste for all the destruction humanity was already reaping on the natural environment. This while my mom's company ravaged Earth's remains for more Dyptherite and terraformed nearby planets with copious amounts of carbon dioxide in the disgusting hope that in the planets' death throes, they too would resort to making Dyptherite.

Now at twenty-seven years old and only alive because my mom was wealthy enough to secure me a ticket to Helix-6 when the elderly and disabled were abandoned with those too poor to do the same, I found myself tasked with aiding her company's research. Which led me, quite incidentally, to developing Lyla out of boredom. I hated working for Mom's company; they stood for everything I hated: capitalist disregard for natural resources, and flagrant disregard for human life. Thanks to the miracle properties of Dyptherite, the remnants of humanity exploded forward in technological advancement, from faster-than-light space travel to cures for diseases, to elemental weapons, and most recently: viable human cloning. The latter was why Mom held human life in a rather callous disregard nowadays; why worry when people were theoretically replaceable, right? I wasn't sure if I believed in metaphysical concepts like souls, but seeing clones go unstable and explode after seven years wasn't a pretty sight – especially the look of terror they all got beforehand. Now from Helix-6 to Earth, humanity had developed a new low: corporate warring. Dyptherion Inc. was the frontrunner in technological advancement thanks to Mom discovering the element first on a surveying trip on Earth, but that didn't mean we were without rivals.

Torq Industries primarily focused on the combat applications of Dyptherite. They pioneered the classification system F-S (F, E, D, C, B, A, S) with F being the lowest damage tier of weapon and S being the highest. Conventional ballistic weaponry typically topped out at D, compared to S-rated guns that usually carried rare elemental effects due to purposefully destabilising the Dyptherite such as electricity or fire. One drop of Dyptherite could create 100 elemental guns but each one cost millions to buy. However, Dyptherion Inc was a very wealthy company, more so than any company on Earth, so

Mom made sure our best contractors, which included my dad, had S-rated fire element guns. Dad was Earth Special Forces, Joint Task Force 5 from Canada. Now he was just a nepotism hire for Dyptherion. I never got to see him because his team was always engaged against Torq forces on one world or another. I missed him dearly. He used to carve busts of Mom and me out of wood with nothing but a pocket knife. We still had some around the house. I hoped he was okay. For all our technology, a nightly holotape wasn't enough. He could die in a firefight tomorrow and there'd be nothing I could do about it. Mom always said to stop worrying, but funny enough, the only time I didn't worry was when I worked on Lyla and she hated that.

I texted my Nana good morning as I always did daily:

—*Morning, how are you? No news from Dad lately and I'm starting to worry about Mom. She's always been a workaholic, but ever since we moved to Helix-6 she seems obsessed. She never minded me gaming all night before...*

—*Morning, sunshine, I'm good thanks, just camping like crazy. I worry about Mom too; she works too much. She needs to relax and let it be sometimes.*

Just then Mom walked up with a strange look on her face.

"You're back early... Nana's worried about you; she says you work too much," I said.

"Don't listen to your Nana, she's crazy. I paid a lot of money to build her a campground on this planet and get her here; the least she could do is not worry. I've got this!" Mom said stubbornly.

Mom always said never to listen to Nana, which always confused Nana and me. Nana wasn't diagnosed with anything to suggest her judgement was compromised, nevertheless, it was always the same: "Don't listen to your Nana." Strange. I owed everything to my mom. Without her, the doctors would have declared me a vegetable and had me put down. They were insistent that I'd never be able to do anything and be a wheelchair-bound nobody. But Mom taught me to walk with a walker and made me learn to write; heck, she fought to teach me everything uphill all the way. Nowadays, our relationship was strained. It took me many years, but I finally realised she wasn't perfect.

My mom really was work-obsessed, but more than that, she was a terrible listener. She'd hear you up until she got an idea of what to do and then she'd be off doing it regardless of whether it was what you *really* wanted, or just what she wanted for you. Once she had an idea in her head, she was unstoppable. I really had a lot of respect for her even if her determination left her spearheading a desperate war when she wasn't even a soldier. I guess I just worried she was finally out of her depth. By the strange look on her face, I began to wonder if she realised it too. After a moment of staring at me like she didn't know what to say, she began.

"Cole, your father... he's dead."

"What? No..." I couldn't believe my ears. Dad was the best, everybody's best friend, easy to get along with. Despite being a soldier, he rarely hurt a fly; he just wanted to protect and help people. By the tears streaming from my mom's eyes, I knew it wasn't a lie. He was gone. My heart sunk in my chest as tears flooded my own.

"How?" I choked out.

"Torq soldier got him on patrol."

Figures, I thought. *The best dad ever was gone because of Mom's stupid planet-destroying resource war! They'd weathered her drinking addiction, they'd weathered each other's obsession with work, but this damn war.... It was her fault!*

"You did this!" I suddenly yelled, with tears streaming down my cheeks. "The number of times he almost left cuz of your drinking, and now he's dead cuz he stayed to fight *your* war!"

"Cole..." she said, shocked.

Nana and I had planned an intervention over Mom's drinking but it was never the right time. Now the truth was thrown at her full force. I didn't care anymore. After a while, she just stormed off crying. Part of me began to feel bad, though I had no regrets; it hurt to see her sad. I felt worse for Dad though, dying all alone in some fighting hole, doubtless thinking he was helping us somehow. Now he was gone... just like that. Our family would never be the same. Some nameless Torq soldier was out there all proud of themselves for felling a mighty Dyptherion warrior, probably lording my dad's special gun over his buddies. I looked down at my wheelchair, then the fires of vengeance died down under the cold, harsh waters of reality. I couldn't avenge him; an unarmed cripple could do nothing against a trained soldier. Depressed, I went back to my room and rolled around for a bit pondering my next move before deciding on a violent gaming session. Nameless non-player characters would feel the wrath I owed that Torq soldier who could be dead for all I knew.

The next day, Mom never came home, which wasn't too weird until days turned into months. I'd resorted to watching the news daily where I learned Dyptherion Inc. had grown more aggressive, much more aggressive, by effectively instituting corporate drafts. Mom was building an army from her own scientists and randoms off the street.

I gave up on gaming, opting instead to do what no gamer dared: go outside. I drove my wheelchair to the outskirts of the city, where I started to notice flyers hanging on buildings. I rode up to one.

Upon reading it, I was horrified. It said:

Citizens of Helix-6,

Join the war effort for Dyptherion today and get your choice of D-S class guns. Eligible soldiers will also receive vouchers for return trips to Earth to collect family. Available while supplies last. Terms, contracts, and conditions apply – see your nearest Dyptherion Inc. representative for further details. My horror turned to disgust. *Months she's been gone and now this?! She swore Dyptherion Inc. would evac survivors on Earth for free. Now she's holding the safety of peoples' families hostage in return for service. Dad would be disgusted...* I thought, ripping off a flyer to take home.

Chapter 17 – Perspectives

Three Months Earlier - Earth

"Davis, wake up!" my little sister Vicky trilled. I stood up, smiling her way, trying my best to look happy despite seeing her bald head. I also made a special effort to ignore the burn marks on her skin. At ten years old, Vicky was an accomplished gymnast and model for textbooks, while I mostly did nothing but play video games at twice her age. Vicky excitedly cartwheeled out of my room and headed for the stairs. The air stunk like rotten eggs today; the smog was heavy in Quebec. I donned my jeans and leather jacket before heading downstairs.

I heard my dad coughing hard before my feet even hit the landing.

"Davis Fington, hurry up or we'll be late for Vicky's last appointment," my mom demanded so I got a move on. My dad slowly ambled his way to the family's two-door car while I opted to hop on Dad's Harley. I'd promised Vicky I'd take her home on it when we got the good test results we hoped for. Inwardly, I was deeply worried for Vicky and my dad. Radiation seemed to drain Vicky more than it helped, while all the pollution had ruined Dad's lungs.

Eventually, we rolled up on the hospital, then rushed inside only to wait hours for a doctor to deign to see us.

"Mr. and Mrs. Fington?" a stout Indian doctor said as he ambled towards us.

"Yes?" my mom replied.

"Come with me, please ..." He led them into his office, leaving us alone in the sterile hall filled with the annoying beeps of ignored hospital equipment.

What felt like hours later, our parents returned. I managed to catch the sombre looks on their faces before they forced smiles. Thankfully, Vicky didn't notice; she was too busy singing out the lyrics in a children's book. My mom leaned over to my ear. "Terminal..." she whispered. I could see she was fighting to hold back tears. I could tell by the warning look in Dad's eyes that it was game time.

"Good news, honey, you're fine!" Dad said. Vicky cheered, then hugged everyone, including the doctor, who looked numb. We were lucky, I guess, that the doctor was still around. Most of the wealthier doctors boarded a flight to Helix-6. I could imagine how exhausting it must be for him to be the one left to hand out cancer diagnoses to Earth's poor pollution-riddled families.

After gathering myself, I took Vicky's hand, leading her to the Harley. On the way home, I struggled to maintain my composure. Dad was dying, and now Vicky... something had to give.

Luckily for me, Vicky didn't mill about when we got home; she just rushed inside to play with her friends. I met my parents in the driveway and we all cried to the sounds of Dad hacking and gagging. Once we could compose ourselves, we went inside. I went to my room to game, opting to boot up *Dead City 7* in the hopes my friend Coaltrain was online. Planet-to-planet internet was still a bit slow, so it took a while for my signal to reach Helix-6 and bounce back. He wasn't online. Bummer. So, I played a solo battle royale match which I lost handily. But during the next match, something caught my eye: a Torq Industries NPC had been added to the game. Cautiously I approached the NPC.

"Join the Torq Industries Fighting Force, (TIFF) today! TIFF soldiers get access to D-S tier guns, and top soldiers gain vouchers for their families to get to Helix-6 and gain access to Torq Industries doctors. Leave your polluted cities behind and journey to the promised land today! Terms, conditions, and contracts apply; TIFF does not guarantee offers to all applicants. See your local recruiter or sign up with me now!" I froze in my seat. Coaltrain had insisted for years his people from Dyptherion Inc. would evac Earth and the news said the same, so we'd waited... but now there was no more time to wait. *My parents will kill me if they find out I'm doing this... I need an excuse. I'm going on a trip maybe?* I thought excitedly. I was a college dropout with little money, but I'd saved enough over the years doing odd jobs, and my family knew I wanted to travel. I'd just have to embellish the truth somewhat. I was sure they'd resist given Vicky's condition, now I'd have to be the bad guy for a good reason.

After I'd packed everything I'd need, I jogged downstairs in a beeline for the front door. Mom cut me off.

"Where do you think you're going?" she demanded.

"Vacation," I said casually.

"Your sister is dying... or did you forget that?!"

"No."

"You can't just leave now; what if she needs you or she—"

"Passes?" I finished. Mom looked at me with a mix of anger and depression.

"You're so lucky your dad's asleep he'd—"

"Kick my ass, I know..." I said callously.

"Fine, just go, but you won't be welcome back!" Mom said, bursting into tears she stepped aside.

Part of me knew she didn't mean it, but it hurt regardless. Steeling myself, I marched for the bus stop, hopped on the first bus to a recruitment center, and rode forward to my destiny.

The first thing I noticed when I got there was how ornate the skyscraper that held the recruitment center was. It looked to have been inspired by a mix of feudal Japan and modernist architecture. Clearly, Torq had money to burn. *War pays when you're selling the guns...* I mused. I strolled into the building and was met by a pretty receptionist in smart business attire.

"Hi, my name is Davis Fington. I'm here to join the TIFF," I said, trying to sound confident.

She smiled. "Right this way, Mr. Fington," she said, leading me from reception to a spartan side office.

I began to feel nervous; my heart fluttered to the beat of a nearby office printer. Inside the office sat a lone hulk of an Asian man with what looked like tribal tattoos all down his arms. I was five foot eight, an ex-football quarterback, but when he stood to greet me, I felt dwarfed.

"Name?" he said in a deep but gentle voice.

"Davis Fington, I'd like to join the TIFF please," I said nervously. The man smiled in a way that calmed me and set butterflies off in my stomach. I blushed.

"Well, Mr. Fington, Torq Industries is always looking for new recruits. There're just a few steps you have to complete:

Step 1: Take the Torq Industries Vocational Aptitude Battery (TIVAB) – a paper intelligence test.

Step 2: Pass the physical examination, which consists of drug and eye tests followed by rigorous exercise. You'll have to complete a two-mile run followed by 100 sit-ups and 100 push-ups.

Step 3: Meet with a counsellor to decide on your career path.

We have a counsellor on site. The whole process takes a couple of days, but we can provide you with food and lodging. Are you sure you want to do this?" he asked seriously.

"Yes, sir!" I said earnestly; he smiled in response and I felt my pants tighten.

Two Days Later

I woke up still sore from PE and marched downstairs to the counsellor's office.

"Morning, ma'am," I said. In front of me was a muscular woman in casual dress. Her eyes betrayed more experience than her attire.

"Morning, Private-in-training. I have the results from your examinations, are you ready?" she asked, pushing her glasses up her nose.

"Yes, please," I said awkwardly.

"You scored a 260 on your PE with negatives across the board for illicit substances. Well done! Were you an athlete previously?"

"Yes. Football and jogging. I used to do workouts on top of that just for fun." I smiled proudly.

"Good for you. So, what are your career goals?" she asked.

"I want to be a top-tier TIFF soldier so I can get my family to Helix-6 for medical care. My sister has terminal cancer and my dad has black lung," I said sincerely.

"Understood. Congratulations, you passed this part of your training. Report to the address on this piece of paper for further instructions."

I took the paper, smiled in thanks and left for the address.

I was proud as the signed sheet of paper called me a Private for TIFF. I felt like I was so close to saving my family, their misguided spite be damned. When I eventually arrived at the address, it looked like an army barracks from a video game, but styled in the same Neo-feudal architecture as the recruitment centre. I presented my papers to a person at the main desk of the closest barracks and they hit me with the bad news.

"Private Fington, from this point forward, TIFF owns you. You will spend two agonising months in speed training and if you survive maybe we'll afford you some benefits, am I clear?" the person asked, who turned out to be a Drill Sergeant. Inwardly, I was appalled. *I don't have two months; Dad and Vicky could be... dead by then.*

"Yes, sir..." I said.

Two Months Later

I'd shot, sliced, exercised, and fought my way through the most tedious two months of my life, being screamed at by Drill Sergeants the whole way through. Of the 100 Privates, eighty dropped out, leaving we most desperate of fools to remain. I wasn't permitted to know anything about my colleagues besides their unit number. TIFF-KJ1 through KJ20. Supposedly, it'd make parting with each other easier if one of us fell in battle. *Clearly, we aren't expected to survive...* I thought when I finally realised that completing training didn't make us anything more than numbers still.

Despite my best efforts, washing as I went, my uniform smelled faintly of sweat and my D-class ballistic rifle shook in my hand like it was ready to explode every time I fired it. *Useless old-timey junk... no wonder they expect us to die. Our armour is barely good against F-class ballistic rifles, let alone this junk,* I surmised regretfully. I'd hoped to be seeing some benefits by now. Having abandoned my holo-phone because I couldn't afford it, I had no idea how my family was doing... was Vicky still alive, what about Dad? Had any of this mattered?

Once more I resolved myself to make it all count as I joined my fellow graduating Privates for a speech from the Drill Sergeant.

"Today my time with you concludes. Some of you will fall while others will make history. I only hope to be around as part of it. Tomorrow you ship out to Helix-6 where you'll face Dyptherion Inc.'s finest. Remember: A win for Torq is a future for your families! Dismissed."

We all stomped and saluted, shouting "Torq" as we did so. Then my fellow Privates went to pack. Having already done this, I instead decided to ask the Sergeant a question that had been burning in my mind for a month.

"Sir, if I may, what must I do to earn a voucher to bring my family to Helix-6?"

He looked at me wistfully and smiled. "Survive!" was all he said.

I was deeply disappointed. *I don't know what I was expecting. Fresh off of training they were never likely to give me anything, but I would've liked a better answer...* I thought annoyed. Little did I know that truly was the best answer. The next day, I boarded the shuttle to the fabled jungle oasis that was Helix-6.

Hours and hours of starlight streaming by my eyes lulled me to sleep. That was, until KJ20 shook me awake. He was a tiny Caucasian with a pencil moustache who looked kind of like a star from my great-grandmother's expensive collection of silent movies from a bygone era.

"What?" I said, annoyed.

"Look!" he exclaimed. It wasn't long before I was grateful he woke me because what I saw out of the shuttle's ample viewport floored me: lush, vibrant jungle as far as the eye could see marred occasionally by a growing number of gaudy human installations. I eyed the rest of my colleagues; we were all wearing standard full-body black combat armour with red accents and helmets with vibrant red visors – standard Torq colours. Only KJ20 and I had our helmets off. Altogether, we looked a lot more intimidating than I felt. I was scared, nervous, doubtful even. *Can I really save my family at this rate? What if only Mom's left by the time I can?* I thought.

I clutched my worn-out D-class TIFF rifle to my chest like a baby for comfort. It looked like a bastardised mini-gun crossed with a deck umbrella with its three rotating barrels and crank firing mechanism. It fired 7.62 rounds at twenty rounds per minute or slightly faster if one could crank faster. I never pushed it, because my poor gun hadn't been cared for very well and I barely knew how to put it back together after two months of expedited training with it.

If I had to rate my training experience, I'd say it'd been sub-par. We mostly worked out and sparred with each other any time we weren't at the range shooting moving targets dressed to the nines in Dyptherion blues. The Drill Sergeant always went on and on about the evils of "The Dyptherion bastards and their cunt leader." All I retained from his propaganda drills was the nugget of truth that Dyptherion *had* promised to evac the poors of Earth but had failed to do so until it could use us as meat for a war effort. However, it wasn't lost on me that Torq had resorted to the same, though they at least promised better benefits in my mind. Time would tell if they kept their word. Moments later, we landed at Helix-6's Torq Air Force Base, a sprawling compound of concrete, sweat, and exaggerated machismo.

I reported to the Sergeant for assignment, then found myself in an electric Jeep headed down a long winding dirt road through the jungle.

"First day?" the driver asked.

"Could you tell?" I blurted out.

"Everybody clutches at their gun like that," she said. I chuckled nervously, then made a conscious effort to right my stance.

"Here, I'm headed back to Earth after this so I don't need it, it'll give you comfort." She handed me a giant cylinder that had a pulsing green light and a single button. "Strap it to your back then press the button!"

I did as she instructed, finding my hands, no my whole body, suddenly covered in a gentle green light that faded away. I knew immediately what this was: a Dyptherite energy shield, and a good one at that.

"Are you sure?! This is Dyptherion Special Forces tech! You could take it home and sell it for millions ..." I exclaimed.

"I know... I did all this for my family, but they died of pollution effects before I had the clout to get them here. Now it's just me, and I won't need the money where I'm going." Her sombre tone worried me a lot. I tried advancing the conversation.

"I'm here for my family too. Gotta save my sister and dad, this'll help a lot, thanks!"

"No worries, I got it off a Dippy corpse. He didn't need it anymore, but a kid like you does."

Dippy was the TIFF nickname for Dyptherion Inc.'s forces; apparently they called us Tiffanys.

Once she dropped me off at the combat zone, she gave me a terse wave then sped off, hopefully to some place happier. I never even got her name. I linked up with five of my fellow KJ unit, and based on their badges, it was TIFF units KJ10 through KJ15. I noticed other Jeeps speeding off with bodies wearing our colours and shuddered. *A shame they didn't have this...* I thought, looking down at my hand covered by a now imperceptible shield.

"KJ19!" a commander shouted for me.

"Sir?" I responded.

"Based on your file, you scored highest across the board among your batch of Privates. Your orders are to take command of the remaining KJ units and flank the enemy base to the south. Any questions?"

"Will we have any cover?"

"Murder Hornets are on site providing overwatch. If there's nothing else, get to it!"

"Sir!" I saluted, then gestured to the KJs to follow. Murder Hornets were a flying troop carrier designated such for their Stinger missile batteries and mini-guns mounted on the side seats. Knowing they were around gave me tons of confidence. We mounted up on an Infiltrator hoverboard and rode off into the dark jungle.

"Okay, lads and ladettes, commander stuck me with leading y'all. Basically, we're to flank the southern enemy base under Hornet cover and take it. Any questions?" I said. No one replied; they all slouched like a punished bunch of children. The music to cover our advance was bullets, missiles, grenades, and the oh so unsettling sounds of death screams. I couldn't blame my fellow Privates for being forlorn. For all we knew, this could be a suicide mission.

"Buck up, squad, we got this!" I tried to sound certain, though I too had growing doubts. It didn't matter though, it was go time.

Chapter 18 – Consequences and Loss

Getting around behind the enemy base with Hornets covering us had been easy. *Too easy...* I thought. We dismounted the Infiltrator then sent it back to base on autopilot so reinforcements could sneak in if need be. KJ15 took the lead while the rest of us took up the rear. I felt bad, because as the shielded one, I should probably lead, but whatever. I was designate KJ19; I waited eagerly to be called upon, which didn't take long.

"Nineteen, I see movement, Dippys approa—"

In a split second, her helmet was blown apart by a bright orange streak which also lit her armour on fire. *An S-tier fire weapon!* I noted.

"COVER NOW!" I yelled as loud as I could before diving behind a thick tree. Elemental rounds screamed by all around me. Thanks to the brief extra training I took, I could tell we were only dealing with one element user and maybe ten D-tier ballistics users. I checked that my shield was full, then made a brazen push up to the next tree to get eyes on. We held a slight advantage, having the huge old jungle trees to shade and cover us, but the Dippys had a fortified position with turrets and sandbags, such that one skilled operator could easily hold off our small force alone.

Worse still, we were heavily outgunned. Our armour could barely handle D-tier rounds, let alone an S-tier elemental weapon. I motioned for my team to push, having waited for my shield generator to pulse green, and opened fire. We took three down, only losing one. I huffed under my helmet, with my heart racing as sweat beaded down my back. This was real. Suddenly a Murder Hornet fired a final volley on approach, which decimated the enemy position leaving only a few standing. Out of the corner of my eye, I saw the elemental user's shield pulse green. He and I were the only ones shielded. I steadied myself. "Fire!" I ordered as I broke formation, charging the elemental soldier. *No one else on my team dies today!* I resolved. Firing wildly, I charged, hoping to any force that my gun would hold up till its thirty-round mag was spent. Thankfully, the remnants of my team grasped my desperate plan enough to support me by taking down the other two enemies.

Now it was just him and I staring each other down for a split second. I fired everything I had left into his shield, then dove for cover inside the enemy fortification. I heard my two remaining KJs shouting as they charged over the boom of their guns. Swiftly, I reloaded, took a single breath, and opened fire anew. He utterly roasted my allies. Over their screams, I saw his shield break and heard a loud crunching sound like breaking glass. Just as my mag began to run dry, I hit him once in the head. His helmet cracked and he dropped like a log. We had done it. All of us dead save me, for just one soldier. *Fucking Dippy scum,* I thought. I took off my helmet and spat in his direction indignantly. Then I looked back at my desecrated team and was overcome by nausea.

After minutes of vomiting, I let myself cry. Once I'd shed my tears for the people I knew only by designations, I gathered my resolve before walking up to the corpse of the elemental soldier. I grabbed his gun for myself; it was beautiful, and had a vivid orange body with a pulsing red cylinder instead of a barrel that opened into an almost flower-like shape. It had a stock like a rifle but instead of being straight in shape, it had a curved contoured body with a single straight-edged indent for a glowing yellow holographic sight. When I inspected the trigger, not only did I notice how normal the assembly was, but right by the trigger on the left side of the body, two names were engraved. *For Cole & Sandy* it said. I stopped dead. My best friend Coaltrain online lived here on Helix-6, and his mom's name was Sandy too. *What are the odds?* I queried. I decided to banish the thought. I attached my new gun to the magnet-holster on my back, then advanced into the base with my old faithful rifle. I don't know why I didn't use my pilfered gun; this just felt more natural.

"What is so important here that they stationed an elemental user to guard it?" I mused aloud, re-equipping my helmet. The 'base' was so small it hardly felt right to call it that. Basic supplies, bunk beds, tactical comms gear, rations, ammo; it was all here, but not much else. That was, until I noticed a retro flash drive tucked away behind a folder. "You better hold the means to end this war or my allies died in vain..." I grumbled, trying not to envision their desecrated smoking corpses. I opened a nearby tactical laptop and gently inserted the drive. What was on it blew my mind. Pictures showing Cole's mom, the CEO of the Dippys, injecting herself directly with Dyptherite, which was a big no-

no for safety, and more damning: direct orders from her to all Dippys to drain Earth dry and continue this war by all means. There was a single audio file so I hit play.

"Ma'am, you swore to evac Earth!" a scientist said.

"I did, but I don't care about that anymore. Like Torq, I just want more Dyptherite, unless people sign on to be soldiers, I don't need them," Cole's mom said coldly.

"Are you alright? Your eyes have gone blood red again …"

"Fine… I'm fine, send the order out that I want all 'Tiffanys' hung or quartered. Dead by any means necessary. If Torq won't surrender their Dyptherite, we'll take it from the CEO's cold, dead hands. Also, any dissenters to this war get a free one-way trip to Earth, courtesy of our stolen Torq shuttles. Do make sure the pilots wear Torq garb. We don't want our share prices to fall by appearing to have any involvement."

With that, the audio clip drew to an end. I vaguely heard something rustle, like a secret recorder had been pushed into a pocket, then the recording ended. Whatever Cole's mom was doing to herself, she wasn't anything like the nice lady he described. She had become genocidal. I grabbed the whole laptop, taking it with me on the long march back to base. Luckily for me, the commander met me in a Jeep a quarter of the way there so I hitched a ride back with him.

The commander's face was grim through the whole evidence showing. "So, she started this damn war now she intends to end it, huh?" he grumbled finally.

"It appears that way, sir. They had an elemental shielded soldier guarding this so it must be true," I noted. I attempted to hand over the gun I'd taken but the commander waved me off.

"It's yours now, ye earned it."

"Thank you, sir."

"You're welcome, Sergeant Fington. We lost many of rank and file today so I'm submitting your deeds as reason for this rank boost."

"Sir, if I may, I have terminally ill family back on Earth; will Torq Industries help me get them here for treatment?" I asked hopefully.

"If they won't after hearing this, I will, Sergeant." My heart swelled; in one mission I'd done what I initially set out to do. Now all I had left to do was hope my family was still alive. My dad would be stubborn; no doubt he'd resist help. My sister wouldn't be hard to convince. I figured once she was done crying about me joining TIFF in secret, Mom would be proud. That just left one thing: my new gun. If I really did kill my internet bestie's dad, I owed him an explanation.

Two Days Later

After my rushed promotion had been finalised, I was granted a day's leave, which I used to look up Cole Sanburg. It wasn't hard to find his mom's mansion. Luckily for me, news of the Dyptherion Inc. secret recording had already gone viral, so there was no doubt in my mind Cole had heard it. The drive had also contained troop deployments, secret memos, and even travel schedules. So, I knew Cole and his mom should be home. I was wearing civilian clothes: my jeans and a leather jacket with a TIFF t-shirt underneath. I figured it'd be best to enter as Cole's friend first, then try to explain the gun I carried. Protesters lined the street outside their home, so I exposed my TIFF shirt temporarily to cheers, which got me through. Nervously, I rang the doorbell and Mrs. Sanburg answered.

"Hello, Mrs. Sanburg, my name is Sergeant Davis Fington, I'm a friend of Cole's. May I come in?" I said.

"Certainly, Sergeant Fington, I'll call him."

"Thanks, let him know I go by Daveed online, he'll understand."

"Okay ..."

A while later, a rail thin guy with glasses in an electric wheelchair rolled up.

"Coaltrain?" I asked, smiling.

"Daveed, it is you; the hell are you doing here?"

"Regretfully, I've come to return this with my condolences." I carefully handed Cole the gun. Near instantly, they both started crying.

"How did it happen?" Cole asked.

"He fell guarding the intel that recently leaked about your mom..." I answered.

"How do you know this; did you fight alongside him?" Mrs. Sanburg asked, weeping.

"Honestly, ma'am, I'm the one who killed him and delivered the intel..." I admitted.

"Whaaat?!" Cole exclaimed, flabbergasted. In response, I undid my jacket, exposing my TIFF shirt and dog tags.

Cole pointed his dad's gun at me, then gestured with his free hand at the front door. "GET OUT!" he yelled.

"Cole, honey, shoot this man for Mommy," Mrs. Sanburg cooed. Her eyes began glowing red, which seemed to unnerve Cole as much as it did me.

Through tears of rage, Cole flung his free arm at the door in a directional gesture. "I said GET OUT," he screamed.

Shockingly, Mrs. Sanburg back-handed Cole, seized the gun, and began spraying wildly.

"YOU JEOPARDIZED YEARS OF WORK, RUINED THE EMPIRE I WAS BUILDING FOR MY SON... NOW DIE!" she screamed.

"I understand your rage, but refrain from firing or your house will burn down!" I tried to reason with her while deftly dodging her amateur aim. Realizing she wouldn't quit, I seized my opening when her mag ran out. Charging, I grabbed the gun in one hand, pushing it aside, and uppercut her with my free fist. Now armed with the family gun, to my chagrin I stood facing a crying Cole and his bloodthirsty mother whose body was beginning to glow red from her veins.

The living room of Cole's home had begun to light up in flames from the elemental gun's flame rounds.

"Cole, Mrs. Sanburg, we need to go, now!" I said, cautiously aiming at Mrs. Sanburg in case she turned on Cole in her rage again.

"No, you go... to hell!" Mrs. Sanburg growled. Suddenly, red energy beams exploded from her fingers, blowing her skin and fingernails off. I dropped to the ground like I'd been ordered to do push-ups, just narrowly dodging the beams which seared straight through the front wall of the house, killing three rows of innocent protesters.

"Mom, stop, you're killing people!" Cole ordered desperately.

In response, Mrs. Sanburg flung her arm in his direction, pointing as though she were about to give a lecture, clearly blinded by rage. In that moment, there was nothing I could do to stop the beam still emitting from her finger from blasting through Cole's skull. Desperately, I rushed forward and bashed her in the head with the gun, knocking her out cold. Despite the blood on her forehead, she looked serene; that was until acrid smoke began to build, obscuring my view and choking me. Carefully, I dragged the Sanburgs from the burning building before turning to face the growing mob.

"Cole Sanburg has died by her hand. I declare this war over and put Sandra Sanburg under citizen's arrest with the authority vested in me as Sergeant of the Torq Industries Fighting Force! Any questions?" No one spoke, but eventually some people cheered. "Death to Dippys!" one man yelled.

Two Days Later

Thankfully, the commander had kept his word, ensuring my family was treated with Helix-6's miracle Dyptherite cures. Though I made certain they didn't use any direct injections to avoid any personality shifts or superpowers like what Mrs. Sanburg had exhibited. In more great news, the TIFF granted me an honourable discharge now that I'd effectively ended the war. I'd heard Mrs. Sanburg had blamed me for Cole's death and swore revenge, but I didn't care. She was in prison for life under special watch by voluntary TIFF forces. I'd opted to sell the Sanburg family gun for a cool three million dollars, which was just enough to buy a modest two-story bungalow – the Helix-6 housing market was worse than Earth because everyone on Helix-6 had to be rich to begin with in order to get there. Apparently, my commander had conquered the Dyptherion Inc. headquarters in the name of Torq then had divested most of its resources to pay families of those lost in the war. He was a good man. Torq wasn't perfect; they were still terraforming and destroying planets' ecosystems for Dyptherite no different than their enemies had, but at least they paid their soldiers well, and even took in Dyptherion Inc units with amnesty. I was glad soldiers weren't basically abandoned to fend for themselves the way some Earth governments seemed to do; not that it was my business anymore.

I had been extremely lucky, sure I lost my only friend and had to live with many deaths, but I'd only needed to see combat once to fulfil my ultimate goal: my family safe and whole again.

"We're so proud of you, Davis... Sergeant Fington!" my mom said, crying happy tears. My dad just shook my hand, then handed me the keys to his Harley, which he'd somehow convinced my commander to bring along. Apparently, it was his condition for leaving. The thought made me laugh, which drew a quizzical look from Dad, but I just smiled and shook his hand in thanks. Vicky, on the other hand, was too busy practising gymnastics to say anything, which was fine by me. We'd all lied by saying she was fine on Earth, so she didn't need to understand why she was actually fine now. I was just overjoyed everyone was proud as well as safe. My mission had been accomplished.

Chapter 19 – Rocket-Powered Coaltrain

"My name is Cole Sanburg; I should be dead," I said to the flabbergasted funeral attendant who'd found me awake on his autopsy table. I remembered everything, right down to my own mother maybe accidentally blowing my head apart. I could see myself in a nearby mirror. All I had to show for my previously mentioned explosive death were a few scars where the lingering Dyptherite from Mom's attack had fused my head back together.

"Is my wheelchair around?" I asked.

"Down the hall, I'll grab it," he said, nervously clutching his Christmas sweater.

Once I was mounted up, I said, "LYLA awaken, code Cole." Moments later, Lyla stood on her robotic projector arm looking sexy.

"Greetings, Cole, how can I help you today?" she said in a sultry voice.

"How long have I been out?" I asked.

Anticipating my real question, she answered, "Three weeks, the war is over, and Sandra Sanburg is currently held in supermax prison under Torq guard. All of your family's assets have been seized and you've been declared dead."

"Great..." I said sadly. *Mom's gone and so is everything else. Other than this wheelchair, I've got nothing.*

Ignoring the stuttering requests from the funeral attendant to stay, I left the funeral home. I drove out into the streets of Helix-6, ignoring the quizzical looks from some people. Part of me somehow assumed that their reactions were because of Mom's famous fall, no doubt including news of my death. People started filming me with their holophones; some even said my name in awe. After a while of silent driving, I finally made it to my house with not much battery left. The house had been repaired from Mom's fire gun attacks and turned into a Torq base. I was ambivalent; I'd always disliked that gaudy house. I just hoped some of my stuff remained. I rolled into the kitchen on the main floor, which had been turned into reception. At the main counter, a lady that looked a lot like Lyla smiled my way.

"Hello, Mr. Sanburg, can I help you?" she said.

"You know me?!" I exclaimed.

"Everyone does; you're the man who survived death."

"News travels fast, eh?"

"Indeed. So, what did you need?"

"Is any of my stuff still here?" I asked hopefully.

"No, sorry, the estate was sold off to Torq."

"Can I check my room out before I go?"

"Sure."

"Thanks."

I rode the house elevator up to my room; it had been stripped bare. I looked at Lyla and smiled.

"Lyla, disengage safe, code Sanburg1," I said.

Lyla flashed blue in response, and moments later, a chunk of the south wall disengaged and swung out. Inside was a closet-sized safe Mom had installed for me. I'd integrated its systems with Lyla years ago in case I fell from my chair or needed a way to get in quickly. Paranoia had paid off. Inside was my prototype battle chair, a spare charger, and a horde of cash from years of birthdays under a rich Mom. The battle chair was a joke project Dad and I had worked on over the years. It had an elemental gun strapped to each armrest, neon lights that glowed red in the undercarriage, and most excitingly, two rockets strapped to the back frame. The whole thing ran on two drops of Dyptherite, thereby negating the need for batteries. I disengaged Lyla's command arm from my main chair, then carefully synced it with the battle chair so she could monitor the Dyptherite and control the chair's unstable systems safely.

I drove my old chair up beside the battle chair, transferred into the battle chair, then started stuffing the backpack above the rockets with cash. All together, I had about a million dollars, which wouldn't get me too far in this economy. My plan was simple: leave home behind for good, grab a new holophone, and if possible – network with other 'zombies', if such people even existed. I hoped others were in my situation if only so I wouldn't be lonely. It was selfish to be sure. I sealed the vault via Lyla, then quietly left home being thankfully ignored by the secretary. *Disabled people are practically invisible on this world* I thought, for once happy for that fact. I didn't know how I'd go about explaining my battle chair if it came down to it.

I hailed a hover taxi and began the journey downtown, covering myself and my guns with a blanket. No one asked any questions, which was good. I grabbed a new holophone from a downtown kiosk then Googled disabled people's meetings. There was one for soldiers disabled by the war taking place in an hour downtown, so I began the chair trek down the street. My scars turned out to be the key to my entry as the receptionist only needed one look at me to let me join, no questions asked.

For the most part, I just listened as I wasn't a soldier, so I had no experience to contribute.

The room was awkwardly quiet till one man with a red bird on his jacket spoke up.

"The rich, the Torqs of the world did this to us. Promised us riches and safety for our families and what did we get? Nothing!"

The room was full of agreement and nodding.

The bird man continued, "They tried to hide it but you know what I learned? Injecting Dyptherite directly gives you superpowers!"

I interjected carefully, "Uh... ya I heard that too but I also heard it drove Sandra Sanburg mad."

The bird man looked at me like he knew me. "What's a little madness in this mad society? We have to get ours. Rumour has it the Richie Riches of Helix-6 have been injecting their kids, especially the disabled – thinking it'll cure 'em."

I groaned in audible disgust along with a few others. Dyptherite cures *had* negated most diseases, but for those previously afflicted by disabilities, there wasn't much extraction-based cures could do. *I hate to admit it, but if direct Dyptherite blasts can bring me back from the dead, maybe they have a point...*

I looked at bird man; he was quite shifty with his beady eyes, nervous demeanour, and greasy skin. The red bird on his jacket was strikingly serene, but didn't suit a man's attire well.

"If the Richies won't help us for all we did for them, I say we take their damn miracle drugs and whatever else we damn well please for ourselves! Vets deserve better than what shit hands society deals for them!" he continued, his nerves quelled by anger rising in his voice. People in the room were voicing agreement more and more. I was beginning to feel uncomfortable.

"Vets most certainly deserve better," I agreed. "Do you intend to run for office? If so, you have my vote!" I said, trying to sound eager enough that his wrath would calm.

"No," he replied ominously. In that moment I knew I wouldn't find like-minded people here, so I quietly excused myself. I'd hoped my eerie run-in with bird man was the last time, but my hopes were quickly dashed.

"Sanburg!" bird man called out behind me. Without thinking, I turned his way.

"Yes?" I said nervously as I shifted my hand under my blanket to the trigger of my left gun.

"I knew it... that's why you warned against injecting Dyptherite, you're the Dippy zombie Sandra made!" he said excitedly.

I cringed. "I'm no 'Dippy zombie', just Cole, thanks. What did you want?"

"You're proof the rumours must be true, you lived!"

"Sure, but as far as I know I've no superpowers."

"Whatever, you're still the man I need to take down the Richies exploiting whole planets for Dyptherite. You know just as well as I do Torq is no better than Dyptherion was! We can take them all down together." His earnest eagerness would easily sway a lesser man, but I wasn't fooled.

"One honourable vet such as yourself and a cripple like me can't do anything to Torq," I said, trying to sound calm and respectful when I was growing uncomfortable and nervous. Bird man seemed overly agitated by my response as if I'd insulted his life-long dream.

"Fine. Bye," he said abruptly, leaving with a dismissive gesture. Glad that our talk was over, I settled my thoughts on where to go next. I was homeless with only what I could carry to my name. I decided to look up Davis Fington and easily found his family's bungalow on the outskirts of town. I figured since he ruined my life, he at least owed me lodging; not that I blamed him for how events transpired per se.

When I finally cabbed my way to Davis's house, I rang his doorbell. A little girl answered the door.

"Hi, Vicky, is Davis in?" I asked.

"Yep, who are you?" she said.

"I'm his friend Cole."

"I'll go get him, bye."

"Thanks!"

A while later, Davis came to the door. He took one look at me, then his face went white.

"How the he—" He cut off, his left hand reaching behind his back for something, then a moment later his body glowed green.

"I'm not here to hurt you, I came to say I forgive you for how things went down... You were forced to kill my dad, and you spared my mom who did deserve to die. You even tried to save me from her. I have nowhere to go thanks to Mom; can we still be friends?" I asked, doubtful.

"Dude, you're a fuggin' zombie!" Davis's shield had faded to an imperceptible light. Though I knew he was still shielded.

"I'm still me, can I come in? If my eyes glow red you can shoot me guilt-free..."

Nervously, he opened the door enough for my chair. I saw a green flash as his shield was disengaged.

Davis's family was gathered around the living room TV enraptured by something. I rolled up behind them and saw my mom and me on the news.

"Tonight, on Eden News: Sandra Sanburg escaped Torq imprisonment with a small group of prisoners seemingly enhanced by her Dyptherite blasting ability. In other news, eye-witnesses have confirmed Cole Sanburg is alive; here are images taken by curious civilians... and finally rumours of Torq CEO Rahul Torq injecting his type-2 diabetic daughter with Dyptherite appear to be true. No word on her condition at this time. Torq authorities caution against Dyptherite injections to no avail as we have reports of black-market sales surging. Tune in tomorrow for any updates surrounding this or other news! Kaylee Jones, Eden News."

"My mom escaped?!" I exclaimed despite myself, causing fearful reactions from Davis's surprised family.

"What the he—" Davis's dad started.

"Hi, I'm Cole, the guy on the news, I'm Davis's friend. Sorry to scare you."

"Oh, that's okay, honey," Davis's mom said. "I'm glad you're not dead, sorry to hear about your parents like this."

"Thanks..." I said sadly, then Davis and I went into another room.

Davis was pacing while he eyed me. "Thanks for being so cool about all that went down, but why are you here?!" he demanded anxiously.

"Like I said, I mean you no harm... I just needed a friend, now more than ever."

"Okay cool, fine, but you should be dead, man!"

"Well, sorry to disappoint, here I am," I said smiling.

"But how?!"

"Fugged if I know, dude, I just learned from the news my mom can give people superpowers. Maybe I'm immortal?"

"Oh hell, and now your oh-so-wonderful mom is out there empowering dangerous people on a whim, and for what?"

"No doubt to build an army. My mom loves being in charge; I'm sure her time in prison only made her love Torq even more..."

"What are you gonna do?" Davis asked, noticing my mischievous smile.

"Fight back," I said.

Chapter 20 – The Finch Takes Flight

"Fight back... how?! Davis looked at my wheelchair, then at me; I could tell what he was implying.

"With this!" I exclaimed, removing the blanket covering my battle chair with gusto. Davis's jaw dropped.

"What the hell, man, you came in here in a tank?" He was incredulous.

"It's just a heavily modified wheelchair: two AI-controlled rocket boosters, Dyptherite powered, with two element-rotating guns to top it off. A little project my dad and I put together as a joke. I never figured I'd need the weapons or rockets, but the Dyptherite power cell came in handy, fast," I explained.

Davis resumed pacing. "So, what? You're gonna take on your super-criminal mom – who already killed you once – and her cronies by yourself?!"

I smiled gently. "I was hoping you'd help, Sergeant."

Davis guffawed. "Fugg no, I ain't helping. I got a family to care for. Torq already tried recruiting me over the holophone before you showed up. I'll tell you what I told them: I'm done with war, done with death... thanks anyway."

"Understood; you mind if I stay here occasionally? I can pay room and board. I just want to lie low a bit while I build a team."

"Sure, might as well, we have two spare rooms. But no bringing your war to my sister's doorstep. The second things get real I want you gone; I don't care!" Davis was adamant. I simply nodded my agreement before heading back to the living room. Davis's family was still wrapped up in the day's news coverage, but on a different network.

"This just in: Multiple bodies were found in the homes of Torq personnel. Warning, the imagery you're about to see is very graphic!"

Davis's dad quickly escorted Vicky upstairs to her room. What I saw shocked me to the bone: Women were stripped nude, their faces ripped off from the jawline up with multiple stab wounds in precise locations. Beside each corpse was what looked like the shape of a bird drawn in their blood.

"All three victims were wives of high-ranking Torq personnel, that's the strongest link investigators have, along with the following manifesto:

I gave my body and soul to Torq fighting their selfish resource war, but now, thanks to Queen Sandra, I've gained the power to fight back, and take what I want. Right now, all I want is Torq faces so they can't smile facetiously at us disenfranchised, abandoned vets anymore! Be afraid, Torq bigwigs, the Red Finch is coming for your families so you too can feel the loss of loved ones like all of us! When I'm done breaking you, you'll be next! Everyone will learn the folly of false promises!

The manifesto was signed with a red bird. At this time, police have no suspects as thanks to security cam footage at crime scenes we know the perpetrator can turn invisible and appears to have super-strength. That's all we have for news tonight, this is John Grandy signing off for Helix Press."

I sat there, mouth agape. *The Red Finch, huh? Wonder if that's the angry bird man from the vets' meeting. Whoever he is, if he does have super-strength and invisibility, I'll need help. Mom has to be stopped. I know she has to be Queen Sandra... who else could it be?* I thought sweating with anxiety. Davis put his hand on my shoulder.

"Are you sure you can't help?" I said with pleading eyes.

"Yup. Super-serial killers are way above my pay grade," he said.

"But you're a Torq Sergeant, what if he comes for your family?!"

"Then he'll meet my guns before he ever sees them." Davis sounded confident, but no soldier could be expected to shoot an invisible enemy. Inspired, I decided to put an ad out on my favourite streaming service, Glitch, for any augmented people who wanted to meet up re: Dyptherite injections and this Red Finch person. I signed it Cole Sanburg, hoping my fame for coming back from the dead would drum up interest.

I awoke the next day to a single solitary message on my post from Jacinda Torq that just said, "I'm in." So I contacted her to set up a meet at a downtown coffee shop for this afternoon. After some begging on my part, Davis agreed to come, if only to assess the situation from an insider. The coffee shop was quaint, small, and almost plain, besides its natural wood decorations. Davis and I sat at a table near the front door, ready to bail if the Red Finch showed up. The shop was almost empty, so it was somewhat surprising when a tall black woman walked in wearing a white dress.

"Cole Sanburg? I'm Jacinda Torq," she said curtly. I introduced Davis while shaking her hand.

"So, why did you agree to meet me?" I asked.

"I found out from a hidden camera that my father's goons have been injecting me with Dyptherite in my sleep. And now your mom and this Red Finch bastard are out there. I want to take them all down," she said seriously.

"Do you have any powers?" Davis asked.

"Besides all of my Torq clearances, I appear to have super-strength, but its use is costly."

"How so?" I asked.

"How old do I look?"

Confused, I said, "Forty maybe, why?"

She grimaced. "I'm twenty. Every time I eat sugar, I get strong but I also get hella old. And you two, what can you do?"

"Davis is an ex-Torq Sergeant and I have an armed wheelchair and maybe immortality. I haven't tested that last part..."

Davis piqued up. "I'm not a part of this, just doing my due diligence for my family," he said suddenly.

Jacinda raised an eyebrow. "Fine, then I ask Cole, what's your plan?"

I tried to sound confident. "About my mom? No clue yet, but the Red Finch? I think I know who he is. I met a guy at a vets' meeting a while back who wore a red bird on his jacket and went on and on about taking what he wanted, just like the news manifesto. So, I'm thinking we go to that meeting and see if he's around, maybe threaten him and if he doesn't fight back, it isn't him," I proposed.

Jacinda laughed. "Great plan, except it isn't. Why wouldn't a vet fight back if attacked? Him retaliating proves nothing unless he happens to have both super-strength and invisibility."

I sighed. "Okay, so what's your plan then?"

"Look at me," she began, "what do you see?"

"A really attractive woman," I said honestly.

She smiled. "Exactly, the sexy, well-endowed daughter of the man our Red Finch hates almost as much as he appears to love stripping his female victims. So, I say we go to that meeting as you suggest and I'll insult the shit out of this bastard to his buddies whether or not he's there. In case that doesn't work, I'll do the same on Dad's news network, just to really make him want me dead. Then you'll stay the night at my place with your battle chair and we'll see if Mr. Big Bird shows up for me."

Jacinda seemed way too confident for someone suggesting she be bait for a deadly killer.

"Are you sure about this plan?" I asked nervously.

"Absolutely, based on his modus operandi, he'd be coming for my body someday anyway. Might as well make it interesting for him. Now, about your mom and her army..." she said.

"After we get the Finch, I say we revise your plan. I don't know if Mom saw the news so she might not know I'm alive, we may be able to get her alone that way," I suggested.

"Deal. Let's get to work," Jacinda said smiling.

We went to the Finch's vet meeting but the guy with the bird coat was a no show; regardless, Jacinda went off on the vets present about the "Bastard Finch" saying that her dad would get him.

With that done, evening was falling, so we cabbed to her place which was an absolute mansion. It was bigger than Mom's with two rows of giant bay windows – one on each floor – marble columns supported a giant balcony overlooking the main entrance, and it had a giant domed roof with a lightning rod at its epicentre. Inside was no less impressive; shining stone floors led the eyes via a pattern in the stone to a giant two-wing staircase adorned with red carpet. Every room was massive. Jacinda led me to the main floor living room since everywhere else had stairs. The living room had a giant fireplace with a wall-sized flat-screen TV above it. Every wall had its own complement of leather couches with little glass jars of candy strewn about on side tables.

"Dad loves candy; if you couldn't tell. You're welcome to sleep on one of the couches. I'll yell Beansprout if I need help, then head downstairs," Jacinda said.

"Got it. Doesn't your dad have Torq guards around?" I asked.

"Yup, but what good are soldiers against an invisible enemy trained just as well as they are?"

"Fair." With that established, it was late, so we both headed to bed.

Sometime later, I awoke to a thumping sound from outside. I'd always slept on a pin and the night was quiet, so it was easy to hear what sounded like someone had fallen over. Scared it was the Red Finch killing the door guard, I awkwardly struggled into my battle chair. Nerves made my whole body tense, so the transfer was hard and agonisingly slow. I heard more thumping noises around the building. I hoped to anyone listening that Jacinda was awake enough to have downed a doughnut or something.

"LYLA awaken, Code Cole," I whispered. Before Lyla could even greet me, I threw off my blanket and whispered, "Battle mode!" I heard a quiet whir from my Dyptherite fuel cell, then the rotating barrels on my elemental guns began to spin up, and finally there was a quiet *whump* announcing that my rocket thrusters had engaged. Lyla brought up a holoscreen to let me pick which elemental barrel my guns should use; in honour of Dad, I picked fire.

I drove up to the giant staircase in the main lobby with my guns locked and loaded, angled up at the middle landing and held my breath. There was another suspicious thump on the balcony outside Jacinda's room; that was the last guard. Moments of intense silence passed where I cursed every little sound I or my battle chair made. Suddenly I heard Jacinda cry out in anger, followed by a loud banging noise. A few more loud bangs followed, accompanied by grunts of effort. I watched the stairs keenly. Just then I saw Jacinda's fist cross into the stairway, followed by loud thumps as a barely visible body fell down the stairs towards me.

"BEANSPROUT!" Jacinda yelled, so I opened fire on the landing while yelling a battle cry. My chair's fire rounds screamed into their target, lighting an invisible man aflame. He rolled around, screaming in agony, which sent him careening towards me on the stone landing below. I backed up while Lyla adjusted my aim automatically so I could keep laying rounds into him. Somehow, the target was still alive, writhing on the floor. Jacinda stomped down the steps, then slammed into his fiery neck with her foot. I heard bones break; he stopped moving entirely.

Smiling, I looked up at Jacinda, then looked away quickly, blushing.

"What?" she asked, confused.

"Look down..." I said, giggling.

"Oh... wow okay... look at me right now!" she ordered.

I looked up her torn shirt until my greedy eyes fell on her exposed breasts.

"See: boobies. No big deal these days now is it?" she said casually.

"Sorry..." I said then opened my pants to flash her. "This is only fair."

This time she blushed. "I guess so, now put it away, big boy. This doesn't change anything, we're just allies, got it?"

"Yes, ma'am," I said with a gentle smile. We pondered the corpse in front of us a moment.

"Is that the guy from your vet's meeting?" she asked.

"Looks right body-type wise, but he's burnt to a crisp so it's hard to be sure..." I answered.

"Let me go change, then we'll call my dad; he has forensics guys who can compare this to the other crime scenes."

Before Jacinda could leave, I grabbed her wrist carefully.

"What now?"

"Jacinda, your hair!" I exclaimed. Parts of her hair had gone bright gray while her face had suddenly wrinkled up like an old lady.

"I told you, my power has a cost..." she said sadly then marched off to her room.

"Lyla, disengage battle mode," I ordered before letting out a sigh of relief. The room stunk of shit and burning flesh. I ended up vomiting on the floor.

A few hours later, Jacinda's father arrived with a full complement of Torq guards as well as a forensic team. He thanked me for helping Jacinda and even offered me some Torq weaponry which I politely declined. Sure, I could've taken it to sell for money, but I still had my million dollars so I'd be fine, plus I'd heard from Jacinda that she would try to get my house back from Torq. Given Torq's history as a conqueror, I wasn't holding my breath.

Sometime after, we were approached by the Torq forensic lead who simply nodded in confirmation. We'd killed the Red Finch Killer. *Guess I'll be in the news again,* I thought.

Sure enough, news crews mobbed Jacinda and I when we were finally dismissed by her father, Rahul, the CEO of Torq Industries. We answered a whole host of questions about the attack, how it made us feel, that sort of thing. Then they asked if I had anything to say. I nodded.

"First, I want to thank Jacinda for doing all of the dangerous work, I was just here really. Second, I want to address my mother, Sandra: Mom, if you're out there, turn yourself in, your war is long since over. If any of your efforts were for my sake, do this for me, or I'll be forced to join Torq in stopping you..."

Before I started crying, I left Jacinda's place, hailing a cab down the road to take me back to Davis's. I felt horrible; I went from a nobody programmer to an accomplice to murder, and now I'd have to fight my own mom. I knew better than anyone my pleas had fallen on deaf ears; there was no way she'd ever turn herself in. In my mind, one question remained: what could I really do to help? Beyond being bait or something, I wasn't sure. By the time I made it to Davis's place, I was plastered all over the news. Davis's family was all smiles when they saw me.

"Dude, you helped stop the Red Finch Killer? That's so badass!" Davis said.

"Yup, now I have to help stop my super-villain-creating mother. Can I count on your help, Sergeant Daveed?" I said, smiling.

Davis laughed. "Been a long time since anyone called me that. I quit gaming months ago. But yeah, now that the Finch is gone, my family should be safe enough that I can leave, sure," he said.

"By the way, why'd you go by Daveed online?" I asked.

"In honour of Ziva David from my fave show NCIS. I watch a lot of re-runs," he explained. My holophone dinged.

"A message from Jacinda!" I exclaimed. "She wants to know if she can come over?"

"Sure," Davis said, "I'd be happy to have a lady as tough as her around."

A few hours later, a whole convoy of Torq armoured vehicles rolled into Davis's driveway. Rahul Torq, Jacinda, and a small army approached the building. Davis and I went out to meet them all.

"Hope you don't mind; I brought a few friends," Jacinda said, smiling.

"Glad to have 'em," Davis replied. I just shook Jacinda's hand.

"Sergeant Fington, glad to have you on board!" Rahul said.

"Thank you, Sir. You know my name?" Davis was shocked.

"I make a point of knowing all of Torq Industry's war heroes. You single-handedly exposed Sandra Sanburg and won us the war. That's heroic to me!"

"Sorry to say, Sir, but it wasn't single-handed. My whole unit gave their lives to win us that fight, I was just lucky..."

"Humbleness is a sign of great strength. I respect that. My men have intel on the whereabouts of Sandra Sanburg, but she's heavily guarded. Not to worry. I brought S-tier electric guns – a Torq specialty – and a new anti-element body armour we've had in research and development for a while. If you're all ready, we can move now."

"Mr. Torq, if you'd permit me, I'd like to go alone to see if I can negotiate with my mother peacefully," I said.

Rahul Torq just nodded, then texted me an address by the Eden city sewers.

Chapter 21 – Battle of the Finches

On the way to the battleground, the cabbie was playing the news, which droned on and on for a while until a special alert came over the speakers.

"This just in: On the same day as the Red Finch Killer was confirmed to be deceased, copycats have sprouted up all over Eden city, all of them targeting Torq personnel and their families. We can confirm, thanks to notes left at the crime scene, that Sandra Sanburg is responsible for empowering these killers and we speculate that she's also responsible for deciding their victims." I grimaced. *This has to stop today!* I had the cabbie drop me off a block away then woke Lyla so she could engage battle mode. Once I was locked and loaded, I took off for the house beside the sewer entrance. It was a decrepit dump. The front door was locked so I blasted it open with my left fire gun and rolled in ready for a fight. Instead, what I found was some sort of bloody orgy with my mom sitting on a throne in a white dress. Red Finches had been scrawled all over the walls and one was even painted on her dress.

I raised my hands in surrender to slow the advance of a bunch of nude men and women who all looked ready to eat me.

"Mom, you have to stop this madness... the war is over!" I said.

"No, Cole, while the Tiffanys still breathe, this war is far from over. Join us!"

So that's how it has to be, huh?

"Fine," I grumbled, then opened fire into the crowd.

Over the wailing bodies engulfed in flames, I saw a crimson light explode from my mom. I focused fire on her remaining allies, some of whom seemed unfazed by my weapons. "LYLA, SHOCK NOW!" I screamed and my barrels switched from fire rounds to electric, which subdued those still standing handily. I heard Rahul Torq's convoy approaching, as did my mom. Roaring, she suddenly burst forth a pair of crimson hands from her chest, which ripped open a portal in the air. In a split second, I saw what looked like Earth, then I was staring at a desolate city with a building in the distance. *Is that the Canadian Parliament building?! It was demolished decades ago for resources!* I saw Mom entering her portal just as some of her Finches began to rise. *You're not escaping!* "Lyla, rockets, now!"

My battle chair launched forward so fast the G-forces glued me to my seat. I opened fire into my mom's back right as the foot pedals of my chair plowed full force into her shins, and we were both sent spiralling into the portal.

Earth – Present Day

In Quebec, a single soldier did their best to lead a people on the verge of civil war.

"You're not *our* Prime Minister, you're a self-appointed dictator! The PM is BM! The PM is BM!" a man in scraggy dress chanted, drawing up cheers and repeats from the growing crowd of protesters. They began throwing gravel and anything else they could grab at the soldier who was covered in red and white power armour. Nothing thrown fazed the soldier physically, but their tone was distraught.

"Fine! If you wish to appoint someone else, by all means, I'm done!" they said seriously then marched from the Parliament building into the garbage-riddled streets. Protesters unsatisfied with their victory gave chase with gusto. Suddenly a crimson red gash ripped open in the sky releasing two bodies locked in combat. The soldier watched as a man in a modified wheelchair shot at a similar-looking woman in a torn white dress.

To the soldier's shock, giant crimson fists burst forth from the woman's chest that pounded the man, chair and all, right into the approaching protesters. The impact killed multiple people instantly. Shock turned to rage as the soldier grabbed their rifle.

As I took in the scene around me and what appeared to be a soldier in red and white armour, my battle chair exploded in multi-elemental bursts. Its unstable Dyptherite power cell had been ruptured in the crash. Even with their enhanced body and power armour, the soldier was sent careening backwards to the dying screams of the citizens that seemed to have been baiting them as we came through the portal. My body smoked among the ruins while Sandra hid in a cocoon of crimson energy for a while, doubtless regaining her strength. The soldier approached us cautiously, rifle at the ready. I must have looked dead as I could barely open my eyes. Sandra, however, was another story. When the cocoon finally dropped, in its place stood Sandra nude, with multiple crimson arms reaching outward from her body. The soldier dodged one of the arms as it reached for them, opting to slice it with their freshly drawn sword. The sword blade melted on impact. Reflexively, the soldier dropped their broken sword and re-drew their rifle in one fluid motion. .50 calibre armour piercing rounds exploded forward, slamming the woman directly, but they only made her stagger.

Without wasting any time, the soldier charged forward, abandoning the gun for some good old-fashioned close-quarters combat. Blow after blow, the soldier gained the upper hand all while dodging multiple impossible strikes from the woman's ethereal arms, thanks to their enhanced reflexes. The woman was backed against a giant tree so the soldier wound up and punched her head so hard her body went through the thick tree trunk in a wash of splinters, which finally rendered her unconscious. Assuming the fight to be over, the soldier glanced over towards the dead protesters. I groaned out of nowhere. Before I could even fully open my eyes, the soldier was on top of me with their rifle barrel squarely aimed at my face.

I looked at the huge warrior standing over me, then at my unconscious mother.

"Wow, you're good... who are you?" I asked.

"I am Strength. ex-Prime Minister of Canada, removed by force. Now I am just a soldier as I wanted to be. Who are you?" Strength said, not wavering in their military readiness.

"I'm Cole Sanburg, gifted with immortality by my psychotic super-villain mother whom you just took down, so thanks!"

Strength seemed well beyond confused, since none of what had just happened was humanly possible. They opted to say nothing. I crawled from my busted husk of a battle chair, swearing the whole way while ignoring the rifle trailing me.

"I need to get her back home; can you toss us through the portal or something?" I asked Strength.

Dave piped up from within Strength's helmet. "Grab those rocket boosters, I have an idea!" he announced through the helmet's built-in speaker. Inside Strength's helmet, Dave guided Strength through the process of attaching the rocket boosters to the back of their armour. Once Strength was done, Dave programmed the power armour to send juice to the rockets and they flared to life.

Wordlessly, Strength grabbed both us Sanburgs under our arms, then blasted off into the portal, leaving Earth behind for good.

I opened my eyes and was shocked to find myself back in the Red Finch house surrounded by nude corpses. I looked up to find Davis there in full Torq gear with Jacinda and her father. Jacinda had clearly been fighting, because now she looked to be about eighty years old. Her father would have to face his own reckoning for allowing her to be augmented, though that wasn't my problem. Strength gently handed me over to Davis while keeping an eye on my mom who had begun to stir.

"I don't know who you are, but that woman is a criminal; toss her on the pile with her ilk and we'll deal with her... Cole, look away!" Rahul Torq ordered. Without question, Strength obeyed. Rahul, Davis, Jacinda, and a squad of soldiers all opened fire on my mom until her power gave way in a crimson burst and she was reduced to ash. All I could do was cry and pound my fist into Davis's armoured chest. Mom's portal closed when she died, marooning Strength on Helix-6 with no way home.

"It's over..." Davis said finally. I just glared at him through tear-stricken eyes. I guess I just needed someone to impart my freshly orphaned rage on. I knew from the moment Mom first killed me there was no saving her, but I never thought it would come to this. So much death was wrought over a war Davis had already ended.

"Who are you, warrior?" Rahul asked Strength.

"I am Strength, ex-Prime Minister of Canada," they said, looking around at Eden city's modernist Asian architecture and clean streets.

"Remove your helmet, soldier," Rahul ordered and Strength obliged, letting their striking female visage and flowing red hair see the light of day.

"What is your full name?" Davis asked.

"Strength," they replied with a soft but commanding voice.

Davis looked at me receiving only a tearful shrug. A kind Torq soldier brought me a chair, so Davis put me in it gently.

"Well, Strength, regardless of who you are and where you come from, Torq is always looking for new recruits. What say you to becoming a soldier?" Rahul asked.

"I already am a soldier, Canadian Special Forces, trained from youth under General Zai," Strength answered with a hint of pride.

"Perfect! You did Torq a great service by saving Cole Sanburg and delivering us Sandra Sanburg. You probably don't even know the scope of your achievements today, but suffice it to say you just saved many lives and ended a decades-long conflict. I can personally offer you a rank of Captain and a team of your own to train. We can also get you new armour and weapons; it looks like yours are quite beat up," he said.

"I'd be glad to train new recruits for the trials! Though I won't need new armour thanks, this suit is one of a kind now." Strength seemed excited.

"What are the trials?" Davis muttered. I just shrugged.

Epilogue

Thanks to Rahul Torq I got my house back, which was great. I decided to rent out many of the mansion's rooms to the poor for whatever they could pay. I even got my inheritance from Mom, given the circumstances, so I'd never need money again. Though that didn't stop me from taking on an AI researcher role for Torq in the old Dyptherion headquarters, which was really just an excuse to use company resources to recompile Lyla for my pleasure. Davis returned home to his family. Meanwhile, Strength was excelling at being a Torq Captain, especially after Davis gave them his energy shield so they didn't have to replace their old armour after all. I'd heard from Davis that Strength's unit was mopping up the other augmented citizens of Helix-6 with great success. Questions still swirled in my mind around the morality and results from humanity's continued use of Dyptherite, but direct injection carried the death penalty now, so no more super-villains should come of it. All in all, I was finally content to live out my immortality the way I saw fit. Better still, Strength's AI, Dave taught Torq scientists ImmortanWire tech to restore Jacinda's youth, and used Dyptherite as a catalyst to avoid the need for human sacrifice. Afterward Strength destroyed the tech and blueprints to protect humanity from themselves. Like the nukes that destroyed Strength's world, some tech just shouldn't exist.

In a tower not unlike the CN Tower of Toronto, but on Helix-6 a woman sat in a white suit with a red cross hanging around her neck.

"Ma'am I have news." A man in a white mask with a red cross on it said.

"Speak." the woman said.

"It appears our augmented units are falling at an alarming rate due to a soldier who wears Canadian Earth armour."

The woman sipped her steeped tea. "Tell me more."

They go by Strength, no last name. Our scouts overheard them speaking of a previous role as Prime Minister... I Fear lady Corkus has been usurped."

"Hmmm. Is that all?"

"No, but how could any of that be possible? The poor of Earth were abandoned..."

The woman smiled, "We live in a world of the impossible dear boy, don't forget we left our children in the Holdfasts to help retake Earth. Maybe this Strength is a descendant of one of us."

"What are your orders?"

"We can't let the damned Keepers get to them first, they're too useful. Keep an eye on them for now. Dismissed."

"Yes ma'am."

Thank You!

Thanks for reading my first full book. It'd mean a lot if you'd leave a review on Amazon, Goodreads, etc. But especially Amazon, doing so greatly helps a book in the endless battle to get sales.

Thanks for your time, I hope you enjoyed my work.

Regards,

Lia Ramsay